W9-APP-052

SEALS

Tynan was close enough. He reached into the scabbard fastened to his boot and sprang, his left hand reaching for the chin of the Soviet soldier. In one quick motion, Tynan lifted the chin and sliced at the throat of the Russian.

As the blood washed over his hand, Tynan pulled backward harder and plunged the knife into the man's chest, up under the breastbone so that the blade cut into one of the lungs, collapsing it. The man's feet shot out from under him, drumming on the soft earth.

BLACKBIRD

SEALS
#2
BLACKBIRD

STEVE MACKENZIE

AVON
PUBLISHERS OF BARD, CAMELOT, DISCUS AND FLARE BOOKS

SEALS #2: BLACKBIRD is an original publication of Avon Books. This work has never before appeared in book form. This work is a novel. Any similarity to actual persons or events is purely coincidental.

AVON BOOKS
A division of
The Hearst Corporation
105 Madison Avenue
New York, New York 10016

Copyright © 1987 by Kevin D. Randle
Published by arrangement with the author
Library of Congress Catalog Card Number: 87-91120
ISBN: 0-380-75190-9

First Avon Printing: July 1987

BLACKBIRD

1

Air Force Lieutenant Colonel Jason Haldan glanced out the left window of his SR-71 reconnaissance aircraft and saw two Soviet MiG-21 Fishbeds climbing toward him. He grinned behind the faceplate of the helmet of his high-altitude pressure suit and hauled back on the yoke. The nose, glowing red from the speed of the plane through the atmosphere, began a slight climb. Haldan increased the throttle and felt the pulsations of the gigantic engines build as they forced the SR-71 higher and faster. He looked out the window again and saw that he was leaving the Russian interceptors far below and way behind. There was a burst of light on the wings of one of the Soviet fighters and a twin plume of smoke as two air-to-air missiles were launched.

"No way." Haldan laughed. "Just no way." He turned so that the MiGs were now in the six o'clock position, almost directly behind him and nearly twenty thousand feet below him. He eased the throttle forward, going to full speed. In his head he heard the engines roaring to life, even though there was no sound from them. The engine noise was being left behind as Haldan burst through the sound barrier once, then twice, and finally three times.

He could feel the rumble of the two Pratt and Whitney J58 bypass turbojets through the seat of the aircraft. He could feel the power thrust him back, deep into the seat, as the plane accelerated. And he could feel the grin spread across his face as he realized that there was just no way that the Soviet fighters could catch him. Even the rumored new Soviet frontline fighter designed to shoot down high-altitude bombers would be no match for the Blackbird.

Out the window, the Fishbeds had dwindled until they were little more than bright specks trailing black smoke far away and far below. Haldan could see the vapor trails of the missiles, but they, too, were dropping away. His plane was so fast that even the air-to-air missiles couldn't catch it.

"Gary Powers I'm not," said Haldan. "You'll have to do better than that."

"You say something?" asked Major Robert Richardson, the reconnaissance systems officer.

Haldan raised one gloved hand and pointed out the window. "Soviets tried again and missed. Not even a good effort this time," he said.

"But they keep trying."

"Yeah, but now we're so high, they've got nothing that can reach us." Haldan looked out the side window where the bright blue of the sky faded into the jet black of space. He could see the stars twinkling far overhead as he reached the threshold of space where the X-15 had once operated. He was flying at speeds the rocket plane could never have obtained. The skin of his plane, painted flat black to inhibit radar returns and visual sightings, glowed cherry red from the friction with the rarefied atmosphere.

"Somebody's still chasing us," said Richardson, checking the on-board radar. He glanced at the ECM indicators but saw nothing to suggest they were being swept by either Soviet fighter radar or the targeting and acquisition radars of the Soviet SAM systems. "Must be thirty, forty thousand feet below us," he added.

"Right at the top of his service ceiling," said Haldan. "Should we go down and bait him?"

"No, sir," said Richardson, suppressing a grin. He turned in his seat so that he could see the Soviet fighter. He saw the telltale flashes of air-to-air missiles being launched. "He's firing."

"He doesn't have the range. Besides, there's nothing on the ECM. He's shooting blind," said Haldan. He banked the SR-71 back to the southwest. He didn't even look to watch as the missiles burned themselves out and began the long plunge to earth where they would crash into the Caspian Sea well away from people and ships.

As they flashed out of the Caspian Sea area Haldan began a slow letdown until he was cruising at only seventy thousand feet. He had reduced his airspeed significantly as they began to photograph the Middle East, taking in Israel and Jordan and Lebanon as well as Iraq and Iran to the east and Egypt to the west. They crossed from land to the edge of the Mediterranean Sea. Haldan let go of the yoke and stretched his arms out over his head as far as the confined space of the cockpit would let him.

To Richardson he said, "I wonder when the Soviets are going to quit trying to catch us."

"Probably about the same time the Egyptians quit," said Richardson. "Three MiGs coming up."

Haldan shook his head and turned to watch. These were MiG-19s, even older than the MiG-21s and without the range, ceiling, or weapons. Haldan felt safe at seventy thousand feet. He eased the yoke to the

left, banking more to the south, away from the interceptors. He kept an eye on them.

"One's firing his cannons," said Richardson.

Haldan snorted. "Even a normal jet can outrun
machine-gun bullets. They don't have a prayer."

Both he and the RSO continued to watch the show.
The Egyptian jets slowly faded away as the Blackbird
outran them while the three jets fired at it with 20mm
cannons.

Haldan's amazement at the stupidity of the Egyptian pilots was cut off by the flashing light from the
flat black box set into the instrument panel, and the
low growl that was building up in his earphones. The
warning light and the low-pitched squeal indicated that
the ECM equipment had detected an early lock-on by
a P-12 Spoon Rest radar. Moments later a second
radar, a Fan Song, swept the aircraft. Or maybe it was
the Squint Eye acquisition radar. Either way, the news
was bad.

Almost before he could react, Haldan saw the dirty
white contrail of the flying telephone-pole-like missile. The instrument panel was beginning to light up
like a Christmas tree as more radar facilities joined
the hunt.

"On the left," said Richardson in a voice that was
tight with excitement. "On the left!"

Haldan saw the second SA-2 streaking toward him.
He knew the missiles were slow turning. They couldn't
match the manueverability of a jet aircraft. Immediately he knew that the Egyptian planes had been a
well-planned diversion.

Haldan jerked back on the yoke and shoved the
throttles forward. The sudden thrust forced him deep
into his seat, and he felt a curtain of black begin to
descend as the G forces from the acceleration and his
rapid turn mounted. Most pilots would have dived

down, turning sharply to break the radar lock, but Haldan's Blackbird could outrun even the Mach 3 SA-2.

As his vision began to clear, the plane jerked violently, as if the back end had been swatted with a gigantic bat from below. There was a howling in his earphones, and the control panel was full of red lights that flashed warnings at him. Haldan immediately leveled the nose and reduced the power, turning back to the southwest as he did so. He knew that the missile hadn't actually hit the plane, but it must have detonated close to it. The real problem was that even the smallest shrapnel damage would destroy the delicate flight characteristics of the SR-71, forcing him down where conventional fighters could get at him.

He tried to neutralize everything by going to level flight. He reduced the throttle even more in an attempt to stabilize the flight path to give him time to evaluate the situation, but the bucking plane demanded his full attention. He fought the controls as the plane seemed to nose over and began to fall out of the sky. For a moment Haldan thought that he had lost a section of wing, but as he applied pressure, first to the yoke and then to the rudder pedals, he felt a response. Then he noticed that the altimeter was unwinding at a rapid rate.

"Get on the horn and alert Washington," Haldan said calmly. "I don't know how long I can hold this thing together. I don't think we're going to make the Atlantic."

He felt sweat bead on his forehead, and his armpits were suddenly clammy. There was an itch on his side that broke into his concentration, but he couldn't get at it. He looked out the window and far below him saw the brown wastelands of the Sahara. The last place he wanted to practice survival techniques was the

Sahara. Nothing lived there. There was no shade and no water. He would be lucky to survive the night.

He took a deep breath of the almost pure oxygen that was being pumped into his face by the life-support system of the aircraft as he eased back on the yoke, trying to extend the glide path of the plane. Carefully, almost as if he feared the SR-71 would disintegrate, he held the nose up, slowly coming out of the dive. There was a buffeting, and Haldan reduced his airspeed to dampen it. He tried to turn to the north, back toward the Mediterranean and eventually England, but the plane refused to respond.

Haldan looked at the map spread out in front of him. The Sahara would soon give way to savanna and eventually to jungle as he approached the coast of Africa from Chad. He would be north of Gabon and south of Nigeria, over the only place in Africa where the jungle made it to the coast. Good territory to hide the remains of a damaged aircraft if he couldn't lose it in the depths of the Atlantic, but not a good place for a crash. Trees a hundred feet tall, more trees fifty feet tall, and then bushes and scrub.

Out the cockpit windows was nothing but blue sky spotted by white cumulus clouds. Far off to the south was a bank of dark gray that announced heavy rain. And back to the north were the Soviet-made fighters flown by Soviet-trained Egyptian pilots, hunting for him.

Haldan held it together for a few more minutes. He had managed to reduce the dive and had even brought the nose high enough to maintain level flight. He thought that he had it made, that the Atlantic was an oasis only minutes away. Suddenly it felt as if they had hit a speed bump while traveling too fast. The plane bounced once, throwing Haldan against the shoulder straps of the seat belt, bruising him. There

was a yawing that Haldan fought to correct, then a
second bump as one of the J58 Pratt and Whitney
engines shut down, the impeller blades disintegrating
and slicing through the engine, killing it.

Directly below him the terrain had changed from
the tan of dried savanna to the deep greens of the
tropical rain forest. Far in front of him he could just
make out on the horizon a shiny line that was the
Atlantic Ocean. Even as he saw it, he realized that he
would never be able to glide to it. Not with the engines
shutting down and the smooth skin of the SR-71 ripped
and pitted by the shrapnel from the SA-2 Guideline
surface-to-air missiles.

There was only one thing to do. Haldan reached
out and flipped the red safety cover out of the way.
That gave him access to the destruct circuits built into
the plane. With a gloved hand, he grabbed the toggle
switch. He looked at the altimeter, the gas producer
gauge, the engine temp gauges, and knew that it was
all over.

Then, before throwing the switch, he activated the
distress signal that was supposed to alert Washington
that he was going down. He looked at Richardson,
who was already preparing to get out.

Using the HF radio, he made a single call, telling
his control that they were going in. He did not wait
for an acknowledgment. He told Richardson to prepare, and just before he threw the switch that would
destroy the plane and all the equipment in it, he
checked the panel a final time to make sure the situation demanded the action. But nothing had changed.
They would fall about fifty miles short of the ocean.

He flipped the switch.

2

The wall was blank. Actually, it wasn't blank like a slate, devoid of features and textures, but blank like the side of a granite cliff. There were roughly cut stone blocks cemented together with crumbling mortar that gave the wall random patterns, and by staring at those patterns long enough United States Naval Lieutenant Mark Tynan could see designs, and by continued concentration he could turn some of the designs into pictures.

He had no idea how long he had been staring at the blank wall. He had started early in the morning when the grass was slightly damp with dew and the sun was low on the horizon, lighting only the top of the old Scottish barn. He had started staring when he could see his breath as he exhaled and the chill of the night still enshrouded the countryside. Now it was later, though how much later Tynan didn't know, and the sun line had crept from the peak of the barn down the roof until it was shining on the top of the wall. By raising his eyes, Tynan could see it from where he sat.

He hadn't moved since early morning when he had sat down three feet from the wall, facing it. Around him were a dozen other men, some of them SEALS like Tynan, some of them British SAS, and a couple of them from the West German antiterrorist unit that was being formed.

All of them knew only that they would face the blank wall for a while, then be told to move to a checkpoint. The problem was that they didn't know how long they had to get from the wall to the checkpoint, how far it was to the checkpoint, or, for that matter, how much longer they would face the wall. It was a brilliantly designed exercise to test patience, stamina, and willpower.

Tynan flexed his muscles without moving his body. He prayed that the sun would climb faster; he needed to feel its warming rays. His body was cold, but he was past shivering. He could feel a numbness in his toes and his fingers, and even flexing the muscles no longer helped. The enforced inactivity was getting to him. He needed to be up and moving, not sitting doing nothing and staring at nothing.

Under him he could feel the wetness of the dew on the fresh green grass. But all he could see was the wall. The blank wall. Not even the insects had yet ventured out into the chill of the morning.

To take his mind off his misery, Tynan tried to focus on his recent leave in Saigon. He had stayed at the Oriental Hotel with Bobbi Harris, a woman who worked in the American Embassy in Saigon. They had spent nearly every waking moment together, Bobbi claiming that her job at the embassy wasn't so important they couldn't spare her for a couple of days.

They had ridden in Lambrettas up and down the wide streets of downtown Saigon, watching the parade of military people and vehicles. They had watched prostitutes in their amazingly short skirts and see-through blouses trying to hustle everyone in uniform, both men and women. They had delighted in meals on the rooftop of the Oriental, watching the sun fade until the night was bright with the moon and stars and the flares of a battle-worn country. They had seen tracers in the distance and heard the rumble of artillery and heavy bombers and ignored it all as they planned what they would do at night, in the air-conditioned comfort of their room. They had taken long baths together, not that they needed to bathe, but for the excuse it gave them to be naked together. They had eaten late lunches and walked the streets and prayed that the leave wouldn't end and dreaded the fact that it would.

Tynan had thought he would return to his ship, which was on picket duty in the South China Sea, when his leave ended, but the moment he set foot on board, he was handed new orders. Additional training with the British SAS in Scotland. A Scotland that was dark and cold but free from the terror of war. The only thing to fear in Scotland was the SAS who had dreamed up the school.

Just as the sun touched his shoulders and Tynan thought he would have a chance to warm up, a British sergeant appeared from nowhere and began shouting, "On your feet. On your feet. To the barn."

The men formed a line at the door and waited to be called inside. Tynan stood staring at the back of Thomas Jones, one of the members of Tynan's SEALS team. Jones was the youngest of the SEALS on the team, having joined the Navy right out of high school—and one step in front of the draft board, Tynan suspected. When Jones could find nothing in the Navy that was challenging enough for him, an enterprising chief petty officer talked him into signing up for the SEALS training, telling him that it would be all the challenge he could stand. The chief didn't mention that it would force Jones to transfer out of the chief's division, and that would mean the problem of Jones would be going somewhere else and the chief would never have to look at him again.

Tynan considered Jones to be a near genius. His problem was that he got bored too easily and, when that happened, tried to make things interesting. Tynan found that Jones was fascinated with electronic equipment, so Tynan assigned him as the radio operator but made the job loose enough that Jones got to work on a wide variety of equipment.

Jones was now twenty-two years old, tall and lean. He had blond hair that he rarely combed. His only vice, other than baiting the lifers, was chocolate. He spent most of his money on Hershey Bars and M&Ms, although he would buy beer when drinking with his buddies.

The door opened, and Jones disappeared inside. Tynan hadn't noticed anything in the barn through the open door, just gloom and the smell of animals that had lived in it. As the door closed, Tynan stared at the rotting gray wood that had pulled apart, creating large dark cracks, and waited, telling himself to be patient because there was nothing else that he could do.

Then it was his turn. He entered, saw three men seated behind a long table set near a couple of empty stalls. There were four-by-fours supporting another level that seemed to be holding straw. There were tools, hoes, a pitchfork, a spade, hanging on the posts. A coil of line was nailed to the wall, and near it were a leather harness and bridle. There were square windows, but each of them was covered by a shutter. Tynan stopped directly in front of the table so that he was centered on the man who wore the rank of a British colonel. As Tynan pivoted to face the men, he felt his foot slip in something that smelled as if it had been left by one of the recent inhabitants of the barn.

He glanced at the pile of shit and said, "Reporting as ordered."

"Strip," said the officer who was seated to the left of the colonel.

"What?"

"Remove your outer clothing. Get on with it, man; we don't have all day."

Tynan reached up and began to slowly unbutton his fatigue jacket.

"Hurry it up, man."

Tynan removed his jacket, looked for a place to set it, but saw none. He tossed it to the dirt floor, trying to avoid the cow and horse shit that littered the mud and straw. He started to take off his combat boots.

"Pull your trousers over them," said the man to the left of the colonel.

When Tynan had removed his trousers and was standing there in his OD—olive drab—T-shirt and shorts and combat boots, the sergeant seated on the right side of the colonel said, "Your next assignment is to get to the covered bridge between Leslie and Kinross. Outside, you will be given a compass and a map. You had better hurry."

Tynan turned and started to leave.

"One thing you'll want to know," said the colonel in a voice that seemed to come from the bottom of a well. "The local authorities will be looking for you. We've passed them a description of you. Of all the men. They believe that some kind of prison bus over-turned and fifteen criminals have escaped." The colonel smiled. "We thought that would jazz up the exercise."

"Yes, sir," said Tynan.

"Getting caught by the local constables does not constitute an acceptable solution to the problem."

"Understood."

"And," said the sergeant, "we don't want you hurting any of the local police. You may do anything short of hurting someone to escape."

"Yes, sir."

"Now get out," said the colonel. "You don't have a lot of free time to waste in here."

Tynan glanced at the pile of clothes lying at his feet and then ran to the door at the far end of the barn. Outside was another British sergeant. He said nothing. He handed Tynan the promised compass and map and pointed down the road. Tynan could see no one in front of him, which didn't mean anything. The SAS sometimes gave each man his own checkpoint to prevent them from working in groups.

Instead of running down the road, hurrying as the colonel and the sergeant had told him to, Tynan crouched and checked the map. He looked at the compass, oriented himself, and smiled. The sergeant had tried to send him the wrong way.

As Tynan stood the sergeant said, "You better hurry, sir. You don't have much time."

With that, Tynan took off running. He leaped over a low stone wall and began to lope across a roughly plowed field, the loose dirt making it hard to run. Tynan had to be careful that he didn't turn an ankle on the big dirt clods. He slowed slightly, watching the ground for pitfalls.

As he ran, trying to make up the time lost in the barn, he realized just how brilliantly planned the exercise was. Hours and hours of inactivity. Nothing to do but sit and wait for the sun to warm you. Maybe on the verge of sleep because of the enforced inactivity. Then, suddenly, on your feet with a goal. Run to the checkpoint. Hurry. Rush. But with no idea how long it would take to get to it or how long you had. You couldn't let up for a second, because that second might mean the difference between success and failure. Tynan had to run full bore because to do less could be disastrous.

He ran up to the next stone wall and halted. He used his compass to orient himself, cross-checking it on the map. He sighted on a barn at the edge of the horizon and began to run toward it, through a meadow that was sprinkled with brightly colored flowers and carpeted with short green grass. He hurtled a narrow brook, slipped on the muddy bank, and scrambled up, away from it. He dropped his compass, scooped it up, and continued to run.

He wasn't jogging, because jogging was little faster than a good, steady walk. He was running with his lungs burning and his sides aching and his feet screaming. He was running toward a large red-and-white barn that was not a final destination, just one of the many points he would have to pass as he rushed toward his goal. He ran up to the side of the barn, slid to a halt, and surveyed the farm fields and countryside spread out in front of him.

For a moment he leaned against the rough, unpainted wood and tried to breathe through the cotton in his mouth and the ache in his side, a pain that radiated through his chest and along his arms, threatening to double him over.

Slowly he unfolded his map, his hands shaking. He got out his compass and set it on the map. On the horizon was a tree line, and in the center of it was a single tree that stood above the rest. If he veered slightly to the left of that tree, he would be on course. He snapped the compass shut, folded the map, and began to run again. Began to run before he'd had a real chance to rest. Before he felt ready to continue. But there was no choice, because he had to hurry.

He ran down the hill, toward the bottom of a slight valley, and began the gentle climb to the tree line. He stopped at the barbed-wire fence, wiggled his way under it, covering himself with cool, slimy mud, and then began the uphill climb. He had been sorely tempted to just rest in the mud. Just lie there for ten minutes and try to regain his strength, regain his breath. Except that he didn't know if he had the time to spare. He had to get to the checkpoint. The sergeant outside the barn and the men inside had all told him that he had to hurry, and hurry he did, running as fast as he could. Sprinting where the terrain allowed it. Trying to avoid obstacles in the farm fields, the meadows, and the roads where the constables would be waiting to arrest him.

In a real situation of evasion, Tynan would not be traveling through open country in daylight. In a real evasion situation he would have to reach a checkpoint, but if he failed to make it one day, the search-and-rescue forces would return the next. He wouldn't be given a failing grade. Here he just had to rush. Time was short. He didn't have the luxury of hiding from the police and the farmers. He had to make his checkpoint or fail the exercise.

Tynan thought that he was doing well. He had slowed a little but was still moving rapidly. He had been able to spot a few of the way points. Landmarks that he had seen on the map that would be obvious to someone traveling overland through the fields. Places that were on his path to the final check. He was on track. Then he heard the wailing, two-pitched siren of a police vehicle and saw the flashing blue light on top of the jeeplike vehicle as it bounced across the field, angling toward him. Far in front of him was the tree line that would mean safety, if he could reach it in time, but the police vehicle was too close and there were no obstacles like a wall or streambed between him and the police. He would be caught well short of the haven.

For a moment he tried to outrun the jeep. He sprinted toward the trees but realized that it was hopeless. Finally he slid to a halt and turned to face the police, watching the blue light on the roof rotating slowly, lazily. He bent double, resting his elbows on his knees, breathing hard. He felt sweat bead on his forehead and then drip down the side of his face and along his ribs and spine. He kept his eyes on the front of the jeep and waited patiently for it, wondering what the next phase of the exercise would be.

As the vehicle rolled to a halt and the siren died, the left door opened and the colonel from the barn got out. He asked, "Lieutenant Tynan?"

Tynan straightened up, brushed self-consciously at the muck that covered him, and said, "Yes, sir."

The colonel reached back into the jeep and picked up a British military overcoat. He stepped toward Tynan, holding out the coat. "Here. Put this on. We're canceling the rest of the exercise."

Tynan gratefully wrapped himself in the warm coat as the cool air rapidly dried the sweat from his body, chilling him. He moved closer to the colonel and the jeep as the colonel held the door open and dumped the seat forward so Tynan could get into the back.

"What's going on?" he asked.

"I haven't the foggiest," said the colonel. "I was ordered to pull you out of the field, out of the exercise, and get you to London on the first available transport at the closest available airport."

Tynan grinned as he climbed into the back. He collapsed on the rear seat and relished the warmth blown at him by the heater. "How was I doing?"

The colonel got in, slammed the door, and turned in the seat so that he could look at Tynan. "On the exercise? You were doing quite well. You would have made your rendezvous point in plenty of time if you had maintained the pace and not run into any problems along the way."

"And you don't know what they want me for in London?" asked Tynan.

"Just that we're to get you there quickly. We're going directly to the airport, where there is a plane waiting. You'll have clean clothes there and you'll be able to freshen up en route."

Tynan closed his eyes and waited, wondering if this was just another phase of the exercise, a phase dreamed up to throw him off balance, or if something else had really come up. Not that he minded at the moment. All he could think about was how nice it was to ride rather than run.

3

The flight to London didn't take long. Tynan had been rushed to the airport, where a twin-engine jet sat ready and waiting. He was hustled up the steps and buckled into a seat, and a moment later the aircraft was rolling along the taxiway to take its position on the runway for takeoff. Within seconds Tynan felt himself pressed gently into the seat as the jet accelerated and then rotated, climbing rapidly into the bright blue sky. A minute later the cabin attendant, a young female officer, approached and told him that he could remove his seat belt.

"I was promised a chance to clean up," said Tynan.

"Yes, sir. If you'll follow me, you'll find a shower in the rear. Shaving equipment has been provided. If there is anything else you require, please let me know."

Tynan stood to follow the woman. She was dressed in a sharply tailored uniform. The skirt was tight across her bottom, and Tynan found himself watching it as she walked to the rear of the plane. He glanced up to see that her fine red hair was piled on the top of her head. He was tempted to pull at the pins that held it in place, but he didn't. She turned at the door and smiled at him, displaying pearly white teeth.

"Anything else," she repeated, "please feel free to let me know." Her green eyes sparkled with mischief. Tynan wondered if he was reading something into her face that didn't belong there.

He put his hand on the knob and looked back. "How long do we have?"

"The flight is relatively short, sir."

"Thank you, ah..."

"Kathleen, of course," she said. "What else would a good Irish girl be named?"

Tynan thought of a half-dozen replies to that but decided to take his shower instead. He opened the door to the lavatory and stepped inside.

He wasn't quite ready for what he saw. It was more elaborate than most of them he had seen on the ground. There was thick black carpeting on the deck. To one side was a porcelain sink with fixtures that looked as if they were made of gold. There was a mirror over it and a towel rack next to it that contained enough towels for a steamroom. The shower itself looked to be molded plastic and was set in the very back of the plane. Tynan opened the frosted-glass door and saw there was a seat in the rear of it and a nozzle that was large enough to choke a horse, with a dozen concentric rings that advertised everything from a pulsating spray to a fine, needle-sharp one that could rip the hide off the horse after it had been choked.

He hung up the British Army coat and stripped his sweat-stained and mud-covered underwear, dropping it to the deck of the plane. He found soap, bars of a translucent amber color, and large thick washcloths, and stepped into the shower. He turned on the water, let it heat, and then closed the door. For a moment he just let the water run over him, warming him as it washed off most of the mud. He soaked his hair, rubbed his hands briskly in it, and then stepped back

to use the soap. He wondered idly what it would take
to get Kathleen into the shower with him. He felt
himself respond to the idea but decided that he
wouldn't try to find out. The British had been far too
kind, except during the training, and he didn't want
to do anything to ruin the good feelings that existed.
Although to have Kathleen washing his back might be
worth it.

When he finished the shower, he turned off the water
and stepped out. He dried himself with one of the
gigantic towels and then wrapped it around his waist.
He stepped up to the sink. Tynan found a razor and
shaving cream and lathered his face. He shaved
quickly, grinding his teeth as the razor pulled at the
whiskers on his chin.

Near the shaving cream was a tube of toothpaste,
and next to that was a new toothbrush still in a clear
plastic wrapper. He brushed his teeth and then looked
for the promised clean clothes. They were not in evidence.

Tynan opened the door and saw that Kathleen was
sitting close at hand, reading a paperback novel. He
asked, "Where's my uniform?"

Kathleen snapped the book shut and dropped it on
the seat. From a curtained rack to the side she retrieved
a carry-on garment bag. She smiled and said, "No
uniform, I'm afraid. Street clothes. These should fit.
You'll find everything you need in there, from socks
and underwear to a nice red tie. Your shoes are out
here."

Tynan reached for the carry-on. "Thanks."

Kathleen's hand lingered, touching his fingers. She
smiled into his eyes and said, "I was close by, waiting
for the chance to wash your back."

Tynan hesitated and then said, "I don't think I got
it real clean."

She laughed. "Nice try, sport, but you had your chance and you blew it. Now you have just about enough time to get dressed before we reach London." Without waiting for Tynan to respond, she turned and started toward the front of the cabin, where the club table and lounge chairs were bolted to the deck.

Slowly Tynan closed the door. I'm supposed to be so red hot, quick on my feet, and aggressive, he thought. And I don't even ask if she'll wash my back because I'm afraid of ruining Anglo-American relations. Christ! What a jerk.

He put on his clothes. Normal underwear, white instead of the OD he was used to. Black socks. A navy blue, single-breasted suit with a six-button vest. A shirt so white that it nearly caused snow blindness. And the promised red tie. There was even a small gold clip to hold the collar down.

Just outside the door, he found a pair of black shoes that were highly polished. He slipped his feet into them and wasn't surprised that they seemed to fit perfectly. Somebody had gone to a lot of trouble to get the measurements right.

Once he was out of the lavatory, Kathleen returned. She took his arm, pressing it close to her, and led him forward. She pointed to a chair. "We'll be landing soon," she said. "Anything I can get for you?"

"Got a Coke aboard this tub?"

"Yes. And Pepsi and Seven-Up, for that matter. Plus a variety of American brewed beers and some American liquors."

"A Coke will be fine—without ice if it's already cold," said Tynan. As she turned away he asked, "Do you know what's going on?"

She moved to the galley, opened a cupboard, and took out a bottle of Coke. Not a can, a bottle. She opened it, poured the contents into a glass, and came back. As she handed him the beverage she sat down, crossing her legs slowly so that her skirt rode up.

"No," she said. "We were called out this morning and told to get up to pick you up. Someone from your embassy met us with the clothes. Told us to make you feel welcome and that you had an important meeting when you arrived in London."

"It's nice to be appreciated," said Tynan, sipping his Coke. "I just wish to hell that I knew what it was all about."

Kathleen looked at her watch. "We should be landing in about ten minutes."

"Well," said Tynan. "Let me thank you for your kindness." He took a big swallow of the Coke and then said, "Would you have really washed my back?"

Kathleen smiled, her eyes glowing, nearly on fire. "I guess that's something you'll never know."

"I think that answers the question," said Tynan.

"Don't be so sure," she said, getting up. "If you'll excuse me, I'll make sure that your car is waiting when we land. I'll join you again just before we touch down."

Upon landing, the plane taxied to a special hangar area where a white Rolls-Royce waited. Kathleen escorted Tynan to the car and then opened the rear door so that he could enter. Before he had a chance to thank her again, she shut the door and the car lurched forward. The driver, wearing a military uniform, didn't even bother to turn around to look at Tynan. He kept his eyes on the road, weaving in and out of the left-handed traffic until he reached the iron gate that guarded the vehicle entrance to the American Embassy. They stopped in front of a stairway that led up to double doors.

Tynan leaned forward and touched the driver on the shoulder. He asked, "What's supposed to happen now?"

The driver shrugged.

Tynan glanced at the doors and saw them open. He reached for the handle of the car door, but a woman hurried down the steps to open it for him. Behind her were two men, both dressed in dark suits. Leaning down so that he could see their faces, he saw that both men had longish graying hair. Their skin was white, suggesting that they didn't get outside often. Tynan then glanced at the woman to thank her and was stunned.

She smiled at him and said, "Welcome to London, Mark."

Tynan wanted to laugh. She had long brown hair cut into bangs that brushed her bright blue eyes. She was tall and slender and had even white teeth. She wore a tailored suit with a two-button jacket and a short skirt and black boots. Tynan wanted to hug her, but he was afraid that the men standing behind her would not understand. Instead, he said, "Bobbi, nice to see you."

She grabbed his hand and propelled him up the steps. " 'Nice to see you.' Shit! Tynan, you should be doing handsprings. You have no idea the strings I had to pull just to get here, let alone get the chance to see you."

"Can we talk about this tonight? Over dinner?"

"Maybe," she said. She pointed at one of the men. "This is Colonel John Conway. He's the military liaison here at the embassy."

Conway was the taller and older of the two. His hair was nearly all white, as was most of his thin mustache, but his eyebrows were still jet black. It gave his face a strange, disproportional look. He had

light blue eyes surrounded by huge whites. He had a
pointed chin. He ducked his head to acknowledge the
introduction and held out a hand to shake.

"And this," said Bobbi, "is Franklin Joseph
Wheeler, the local spook."

Although shorter than Conway, he weighed a good
fifty pounds more, about two-twenty. Tynan couldn't
tell if it was fat or muscle, and since he couldn't tell,
he opted to believe that it was muscle. The man had
salt-and-pepper hair, thick eyebrows, and long side-
burns. He had a rounded face with a scar that dived
into an eyebrow and seemed to cross the eyelid and
resurface on his cheek.

To Bobbi, Wheeler said, "I wish you wouldn't call
me the local spook." He held out a hand to be shook
and then smiled. "Although I guess I am. CIA case
officer."

"Let's get out of this wind," said Bobbi as she
gestured at the doors.

They moved up the steps and into the embassy
building. Since it wasn't a public entrance, they didn't
have to pass a Marine guard. They entered a long,
partially lighted corridor. They passed a half dozen-
closed doors that had nothing written on them. Finally
Bobbi opened one and stepped back so that Conway
could lead the way down the stairs.

They came to another long corridor. There was an
iron gate blocking the way with an armed Marine
guard on the other side of it. He stood and saluted
Conway and said, "Is this Lieutenant Tynan?"

"Yes. I'll vouch for him."

The guard opened the gate and stepped aside. As
Tynan started through, Bobbi caught his arm and said,
"I'll meet you upstairs later. If you have the time, I'll
let you buy me a dinner. Or better yet, maybe I can
get the embassy to spring for it."

Tynan said, "All right." There was more that he wanted to say, but none of it that could be accomplished in a few words. He wanted to ask what was happening, but he knew that in a few minutes he would understand exactly what was going on. He followed Conway down the corridor and stopped outside a door when Conway took out a key. Tynan glanced back and saw Bobbi standing at the iron gate, watching him.

Conway opened the door and waved Tynan in. He saw it was a small conference room. He had to take two steps down to it. A medium-brown carpet covered the floor and climbed the walls to the ceiling, which contained subdued lighting recessed into it. There was a small conference table that was highly polished, surrounded by six high-backed, plush blue armchairs. There was a screen at one end of the room that seemed to be hung on the wall like a giant picture but that had descended from the ceiling, and a 16mm movie projector at the other, a film already loaded in it.

"Have a seat, Lieutenant," said Conway. "Would you care for something to drink?"

Tynan sat down and rocked back. He laced his fingers across his stomach and wished that someone would ask him if he wanted something to eat. He hadn't eaten anything in twenty-four hours, and the last meal had been rather skimpy. He and Jones had trapped an undernourished rabbit during a survival segment of the exercise and had managed to cook and eat it. It hadn't been enough though. He could have eaten two rabbits. Now, everyone wanted to give him something to drink, but no one mentioned food except Harris, and she wasn't around. He could wait though. That he did know. He had learned it during the exercise.

In answer to Conway's question, he said, "Coke, if you have it. Seven-Up if not."

When Conway set the crystal glass brimming with Coke in front of Tynan, he asked, "Do you know why we've gone to so much trouble to get you here?"

Tynan shook his head. He glanced at Wheeler, who had followed them in and closed the door, locking it.

"I have a short film to show you," said Conway, "and then I'll ask you a question. We'll play it by ear from there. Please remember that the information in the film you are about to see is classified as secret and cannot be released to foreign nationals."

Tynan nodded his understanding but wondered why they had left the film alone in the room. Then he remembered the guard at the gate who had logged him through. He would not let anyone who was not authorized through the gate. The classified film was as safe as if it had been locked in a vault.

Conway flipped a switch on the projector as Wheeler turned off the overhead lights. Tynan was treated to a full-color version of the Air Force crest and then a warning that the film had been classified and was not to be discussed.

The film opened on an empty runway. The heat was shimmering and the sky was cloudless. Twin black lines appeared, and then the whole center of the screen was obliterated by the sudden appearance of a flat black airplane that looked curiously disk-shaped. The view changed to the side. The aircraft was long and flattened. It raced down the runway and leaped into the sky, climbing upward rapidly, almost like a rocket that had been launched from Florida.

The narrator said, "The SR-71, known as the Blackbird, is one of the most amazing aircraft ever built on the planet Earth. It can cruise faster, fly higher, and outclimb anything."

Tynan stared at the pictures of the Blackbird in flight. It was a graceless-looking airplane that somehow seemed at home in the high sky, flying in the rarefied atmosphere where friction was not the problem it was closer to the ground. Tynan listened as the narrator continued to pour out facts about the plane. In a tail chase situation, it could outrun even the air-to-air missiles fired at it by interceptors, provided the interceptors could get high enough to fire at it. In an hour it could photograph a hundred thousand square miles, and its mission could last for three hours without refueling. There was a version that could carry eight Hughes AIM-47 Falcon air-to-air missiles. The narrator explained that the missiles were slowly being replaced by the AIM-54.

The film went on to explain that the Blackbird, in its reconnaissance role, carried a wide variety of cameras, radars, and other sensing gear. There was a lot of technical material about the reconnaissance mission and a little more about the operation of the aircraft. The one fact that jumped out at Tynan was that the Blackbird, even when operating at the highest altitudes, would get so hot from friction that it would stretch. The pilot and the reconnaissance systems officer were required to wear pressure suits designed to the same specifications as those worn by astronauts.

The film ended with another warning about the contents being classified. As the lights came on, Tynan picked up his Coke and drank deeply. Wheeler moved to one of the chairs and sat down as Conway rewound the movie.

"Well?" said Wheeler.

"Impressive," responded Tynan. "Most impressive. I didn't know anything like it existed." He smiled and added, "It might explain the flying-saucer sightings."

"It certainly explains some of them," said Wheeler, "but that's not the point here. The point is that the SR-71 is so special that when the production run was completed, all the molds and dies were destroyed. All the secret production specs were destroyed. No more of them will be built by anyone, including the United States."

Conway joined them at the table. "Everything about the Blackbird is classified," he said. "It was tested in secret, and when it was finally announced, we caught everyone off guard. They had no idea we had such an aircraft."

Tynan nodded and drank more of the Coke. Carefully he set the glass on the high gloss surface of the table and said, "What has this to do with me?"

"We lost one."

Tynan turned to Wheeler and said, "What?"

"We lost one. Late yesterday. We want you to go in and blow it up. Completely. Totally. So that there are only little pieces of it scattered over a hundred square miles."

"Now wait a minute," said Tynan. "I'm not qualified to do anything like that."

Conway interrupted. "I thought all you SEALS guys were demolitions experts."

"We have training in demolitions work, but what you want calls for a specialist. Someone who has trained only in the destruction of objects. My training has been a little bit more general."

"Okay," said Conway. "How many people do you need, and how soon can you get going?"

"Wait a minute," said Tynan, holding up a hand. "I haven't the faintest idea what you want."

"We want you to go in and blow up the airplane. As simple as that."

Tynan picked up the Coke to buy himself some time. He sipped it and said, "From what you've said, I'd need just one guy. But there are—"

"Okay. Give us a name," said Wheeler, pulling a notebook from his pocket.

Tynan sighed and rubbed his forehead as if he were getting a headache. One minute he was sitting in the chilly dawn of Scotland, the next he was showering on a jet, and right after that he was watching a classified film in the American Embassy. Now, suddenly, he was trying to design a team for a mission that he knew nothing about.

"Before I give you a name, I need a few more facts. Where is the airplane now?"

"It crashed into the jungle yesterday," Wheeler said, "and we want you to destroy it before anyone gets a chance to look at it."

"Just wait a minute here," said Tynan. "Isn't there something that you're leaving out? If it crashed into the jungle, why don't you just drop a couple of your superspooks in and blow it up? You don't need me or any other demolitions experts or anything else."

"Lieutenant Tynan," said Conway, "we don't have time to get into things like that. We have to get the ball rolling. Right now."

"That was Custer's attitude at the Little Bighorn," said Tynan. "Charge right in and get the ball rolling."

"Tynan," snapped Conway, "you were not brought in here to criticize."

"That's right. But if I'm to make any useful contributions, I'm going to have to understand exactly what is going on. I mean, from what you've told me, you need one guy and a parachute. You don't need me or anyone else with my specialized training. You need a mad bomber."

"All right," said Wheeler, holding up a hand as if
to pat the air. "All right. Here's the deal. The plane
crashed yesterday. Both the pilot and the RSO bailed
out after setting the self-destruct circuits. They did not
see the plane explode. They saw it crash into the jungle. Both were later rescued. Washington confirmed
that the plane did not blow up. We have ways of
monitoring that. Now, we want you to go in and
destroy the aircraft."

"I still don't understand exactly what you need me
for," said Tynan.

"The location is jungle. You're familiar with operating in a jungle environment. And the country isn't
exactly aligned with the West. It's more under the
influence of the Soviet Union and the Communist
bloc."

"Ah," said Tynan. " So you're worried about the
Russians getting to the Blackbird before you can get
in there and destroy it."

"That's exactly why we're in such a hurry."

"Six men," said Tynan. "At a minimum. Each
must be armed. No radio, for two reasons. One, they
weigh too much, and two, you wouldn't want the bad
guys monitoring our broadcasts. A predesignated
resupply drop zone and a predesignated extraction
point with a backup plan. How far is the crash site
from the coast?"

Wheeler ignored the question. "You presume a
great deal, Lieutenant Tynan."

"I'm taking my cues from you. You said there
wasn't a great deal of time. I have given you the basics
for a mission without any of the details that I would
need to supply the proper plan. And I still don't understand why you would yank me out of the field when
you have your own operatives available."

"Because," said Wheeler, "we don't want the Soviets to know exactly what we're doing. If we mobilize a force of our own men, most of whom are not experienced in the jungle, the Russians are going to notice. If we go outside the agency, then the Soviets may not notice. We may be able to get in and out without the Russians making any waves about it. We may get in and out before the Soviets get a team in."

Tynan nodded and then stood. "I can see no reason to continue here. If you want me to arrange something, I'm going to need more details. Location of the crash, distances from coastlines and cities, terrains, local populations, government affiliations, and any local help that might be available. Just about everything. I cannot sit here and speculate. I say six men, minimum. Equipment to blow up the plane. But what about weapons? In a hostile environment I would want the new M-16s, maybe a couple of LAWS. In a neutral country I might want just pistols to shoot poisonous snakes and bandits. Without that, I can't tell you what I'll need."

Conway had been sitting back in his chair, his fingers tented under his chin as he listened. He said, "You know, you are not the only man available for the job. We might just find someone a little more cooperative."

"Then by all means do so," said Tynan. "If you can find someone who knows his business and will work in the vacuum you want to maintain, then go right ahead, and more power to you."

Wheeler got slowly to his feet. He glanced at his watch and said, "Lieutenant, report back here in three hours and we'll have a complete briefing ready for you. Please be prepared to list the equipment you'll need and the men you'll want to take with you. If you

can, we would like the current address and military
status of each man.''

''It'll be difficult to make up the lists of equipment
and men,'' said Tynan.

''You have the general outline. Work from that. As
the specifics are filled in during the briefing, you can
add to it and subtract from it.''

''That sounds reasonable.''

Conway stood. He opened the door and said, ''I'll
escort you upstairs. We'll have Ms. Harris arrange a
pass and an ID for you, and she'll be able to help
with anything else you might need.''

''Yes, sir.''

4

Soviet Army Captain Vladimir Stepanovich Molodin sat quietly in the rear of the AN-22 Cock transport plane, his hands clasped together tightly as he fought to keep from throwing up. He didn't like flying, even in the newest of the Soviet planes and even in the Aeroflot version that had seats for passengers rather than webbing for paratroopers. It was the reason that he had joined the Army and not the Air Force. He didn't want to be near airplanes, but even in the Army he found himself riding in the back of them more than he cared to.

Now, after fifteen years in the Army, he had realized that he was going to have to fly a great deal. Armies no longer marched into battle. They flew into it. They rode in the back of airplanes and helicopters, letting someone else, the pilots and navigators, guide their destiny, protect their lives, as they made their way to the battlefront. Once on the ground, Molodin could control his own fate, but in the air, where he was spending too much of his time, someone else, someone he didn't know, was in control.

Scattered around him were his handpicked team. Some of them, like Sergeant Major Grigori Kudira, were professional soldiers who had spent years in training. Others, like Stepan Dobrynin, were young

men who had only recently completed their initial
training but who had shown great aptitude for the military. Still others, like the light-haired, thin young
man who was talking to one of the pilots, was an
engineer of some kind. He was going to look at the
American aircraft that had crashed in the African jungle. He was going to learn the secrets of the plane and
take them back to the Soviet Union.

Molodin glanced to his left where his second in
command, Lieutenant Viktor Krothov, sat. Krothov
was a thin man, almost to the point of emaciation, but
he had an incredible physical strength. Molodin could
never figure out whether the strength was more endurance or physical ability. He had seen Krothov lift
weights that were nearly impossible for the ordinary
man, and he had seen him run most of a company
into the ground without breathing hard. Krothov also
had bizarre looks. He had a long thin face with the
features squished together in the center. He had thick
black eyebrows that met over the bridge of his nose.
His eyes were dark brown and seemed to glow from
the center of his face.

Molodin knew that Krothov was a deadly man in a
fight. He had seen him cut down two Angolan rebels
with automatic-weapons fire and then calmly stroll out
to where they lay and cut their throats to make sure
that they were dead. Krothov would do everything in
his power to make sure that the mission was accomplished.

Seated next to him was Sergeant Dimitri Inonova,
the radio operator. He was the only man Molodin had
not picked. He had been told that the small man was
the best radio operator in the world. If the set was not
working, Inonova could, with a knife and items picked
up from the jungle, construct a set that would work.
Inonova had straight black hair, yellowish skin, and

eyes that were almost oval, giving him an Oriental look. Molodin believed that Inonova came from southern Siberia where the Chinese and the Russian races mixed.

The remaining five men were privates. They were men who had been in trouble during the garrison duty that they claimed bored them senseless, men who had wanted to do something other than polish boots and buttons and prepare for inspections. Each had a military career that had been marked by peaks and valleys. Mikhail Pankovski, for example, had been a sergeant in Angola. He had personally sneaked into the camps of the rebels and cut the throats of six of them as they slept. But once back in the Soviet Union, he had become a drunk who picked fights with everyone. Molodin was glad to have him on the mission because he was deadly.

Seated behind the soldiers, in large, newly covered seats, were fifteen scientists and engineers. Molodin didn't like taking them into the jungle. He didn't know how they would react to the stress of the jungle, but he also knew, from his briefing just before takeoff, that he was not qualified to examine the American plane that had crashed. He had been told enough to know that it was a truly amazing aircraft and that the secrets it held could increase Soviet technology a hundredfold. New metal alloys. Microchips, a term he didn't understand until he was told that one microchip could replace a dozen, two dozen bulky vacuum tubes.

There wouldn't be a problem with the mission, he had been told. They were landing in territory that, while not completely friendly, would be cooperative on this. Soviet aid in the form of food, medicine, and weapons had purchased that cooperation. Anything that they needed would be supplied or could be purchased from the local government. For Molodin and

his men, it would be like a vacation outside the Soviet
Union, with a little bit of hiking thrown in so that they
could maintain their competitive edge. Molodin turned
so that he could see the scientists and engineers again.
The movement made his stomach tumble and his head
spin, and he wished that he had remained still. Sweat
popped out on his forehead and he was suddenly,
uncomfortably hot. He reached for one of the air vents
so that he could divert the stream of cool air to his
face. He rocked back in his seat and clamped his teeth
shut, telling himself that he would not be sick, he
would not throw up.

He had to divert his mind from the boiling in his
gut. The scientists, he thought. Those damned skinny,
overweight, or out-of-shape men who were suppposed
to walk through the jungle. And women. Two women
who had probably never been outside in their lives.
Pale, skinny women, who looked as if they were not
excited about the prospect of living in the jungle for
several days or perhaps weeks.

There was a quiet ringing of a bell and then a warning that it was time to buckle the seat belts. The man
who had been talking to the pilot eased his way back,
smiled broadly at Molodin as if they shared some
secret in common, and then disappeared into the midst
of the scientists. Molodin didn't turn to watch him;
he kept his eyes forward, hoping they would land
before he lost the fight with his stomach.

Over the sound of the engines, he heard the landing
gear lowered. It was a high-pitched servo whine that
Molodin had long ago learned heralded the end of his
ordeal. He felt the plane bounce and rock because the
wheels were not aerodynamic, but he didn't care about
that. He knew that he would be on the ground in
moments.

Then he felt the landing gear contact the runway, felt the plane bounce once, again, and settle to the ground. He leaned forward, against the restraint of his seat belt, his elbows on his knees, his hands clasped tightly, the knuckles white. For an instant he thought that he wouldn't make it, that he would throw up, but the bubbling in his belly passed as the plane rolled to a stop in front of a tan, two-story building that had a glassed tower on top of it.

Around him the men, and the two women, were starting to get up, preparing to exit. Molodin sat quietly, waiting, the sweat drying on his face as his stomach slowed down and nearly stopped its fluttering. He leaned back, closed his eyes, and wiped his hand across his face.

Krothov, who was standing, leaned down and asked, "Are you feeling ill, Captain?"

Opening one eye, Molodin smiled weakly and said, "No. I am fine. Just fine."

"What are the plans?" asked the lieutenant.

"You detail one man to supervise the off-loading of the equipment. You have another escort the civilians into the building and have them wait. I will try to find our liaison here and learn what I can from him."

"Yes, sir."

Molodin closed his eyes, wishing that he could go to sleep, and then opened them. He watched as the flight engineer or the load master opened the hatch to the outside. Molodin was nearly overwhelmed by the sudden blast of tropical air. The plane had been air-conditioned, but now the warm, moist air of the jungle flooded in. The sweat that had dried sprang back, and in seconds Molodin's shirt was soaked, ragged stains under his arms and down his back.

Outside, it was no better. There was no breeze, just the lifeless, heavy air that threatened to smother the men and women. Molodin held a hand up to block the stinging rays of the bright afternoon sun as he clawed at his pocket, searching for his sunglasses. He slipped them on, blinking rapidly. He descended the stairs to the ground. Although the runway had been paved, the ramp area was not. Molodin stepped onto the hard-packed dirt that had dried into a mosaic pattern of cracked earth.

The two-story building that he had seen from the plane was apparently the terminal building. It was made of sand-colored brick. There were large, tinted glass windows in the front of it, and Molodin was struck by the incongruity of the modern flight facility in the middle of a Third World jungle. Parked to one side of the building were two dung-colored Land-Rovers. A flag flew from a short pole near the building.

Off to the left were two metal hangars, both seeming to glow under the sun. Molodin could see that something was painted on the side of one, but he couldn't read it because of the bright light. A small twin-engined, propeller-driven aircraft was parked in front of the closest hangar, and two men were working on one of the engines. They had an access hatch up and each had a hand inside it. A wind sock hung limp on top of the farthest building. Behind it Molodin could see a line of black clouds that warned of rain soon.

The jungle seemed to sweep right up to the edges of the runway, the taxi and ramp areas, and nearly to the base of the building. Tall palms stretched toward the bright blue sky directly overhead. Shorter trees reached two-thirds of the way up the palms, and the ground was cluttered with thick bushes. Vines hung from the branches of the trees. Molodin could see some movement in the jungle. Brightly colored birds that screamed at one another. Monkeys swinging by.

As he stood there, studying his surroundings, a tall black man left the terminal building. Molodin saw him and turned. His skin was so black that it was nearly blue. He had short, curly black hair. The man was wearing a military uniform, khaki with rust-colored insignia on the shoulders and dark rings around the sleeves. He wore a high-peaked billed cap, a black leather Sam Browne belt, and black boots, highly polished. In his hand he carried a riding crop. As he approached he touched the bill of his cap with the crop and said, in English, "Captain Molodin, welcome to my country."

Although Molodin understood English, he pretended that he didn't and responded in French. "Is there somewhere that we can talk out of the heat?"

The man held out a hand, pointing at the terminal. "Inside is much more pleasant," he said in French that was almost impossible to understand.

Molodin turned and strode to the door, waited as the black man opened it, and then entered. He stopped just inside, facing the waiting area that was typical of small airports. A ticket corner at one end, molded plastic chairs in rows, and a small, glassed-in snack bar. It was hardly the kind of terminal that Molodin expected in a Third World nation, especially away from the capital city.

The black man turned to the right and led Molodin to an office set in the corner. The furnishings, an old, beat-up metal desk, a couple of ratty-looking chairs in mismatched fabric, and a scarred table, didn't belong in the new building. The floor was polished hardwood.

The man gestured at one chair, set his riding crop on the desk, and then sat in the other. He said, in his heavily accented French, "What is it that you want?"

"Have you been briefed by your government?" asked Molodin.

"I only know that you and your men were coming in and that I was to cooperate," said the man.

"I am looking for the remains of a plane that crashed in the jungle near here a couple of days ago. My men and I need to find it so that we can examine it."

The man put the tips of his fingers together and rested his chin on them. He nodded his understanding and said, "I have heard reports about it."

"Then you can lead us to it?"

"Ah no," said the man. "I have merely heard reports. I can have my men interview some of the villagers and see if they know any more, but I do not know where the plane is located."

Molodin stood. "You do what you must. I will get my men organized so that we can begin our own search. Do you have any helicopters available?"

"There are two in the capital," said the man, "but they are for use by the president."

"Maybe you can check with the authorities there and see if they will allow us the use of one of the aircraft."

The man got to his feet and said, "Yes, I shall do that."

At the door, Molodin hesitated. He said, "You do know what you're looking for?"

"Captain," said the man, using Molodin's title for the first time, "I may have been posted to a desolate part of my country that does not contain all the modern conveniences to which you have grown accustomed, but I am familiar with aircraft. I do know what we are looking for."

"My apologies," said Molodin. "I merely meant to ask if you were familiar with the type of aircraft. It was painted black, not silver like so many we see. It had a delta-type wing and a dual tail. It varies from the normal aircraft."

The man smiled for the first time, showing white teeth that seemed to glow in contrast to his skin. "I see your problem. Do you know about where the plane went down?"

"I will meet with my advisers," said Molodin, "and secure a map. I can give you the general location."

The man opened the door. "Give me twelve hours, and I may have something for you."

Now Molodin smiled. "I will use the time to get my people ready to go. Shall we say at first light tomorrow?"

"I will be ready then." The black man walked off, having never told Molodin his name or his rank.

Molodin left the office and went to find his men. Krothov was seated in one of the molded plastic chairs, reading a book about the Russian Revolution. Molodin slipped into the seat next to him and said, "Is everything ready?"

"We could move out in fifteen minutes," said Krothov, "if that was necessary."

"It may be," said Molodin. "The Americans are not going to sit by and let us walk up to their prized airplane."

Krothov snapped his book shut and turned to face the captain. "Why do you say that? Was there something in your briefing about it?"

"No," Molodin admitted. "But think about it. It is a supersecret aircraft. They are not going to want us to find it, so it stands to reason that they are going to put someone into the field to stop us. To find the plane first and destroy it.''

''Yes.'' Krothov nodded. ''That makes sense. Did you hear something that makes you worry about the Americans?''

''No, and that is what frightens me.''

5

Tynan sat across the nearly antiseptic white of the tablecloth, looking through a forest of brightly colored flowers, watching Bobbi Harris tear into the steak dinner. She had already demolished a salad, soup, and most of the baked potato. Tynan had been sipping the wine and nibbling at his meal, for some reason not very hungry.

He had been thinking about the job coming up. He was trying to figure out, with virtually no information, the size and composition of the team he was going to need. He would take Jones because he knew the man. He would want Sterne and Boone, two men who had been on the training mission into South Vietnam. Both had proved to be resourceful in a fight, and both had proved to be brave. Neither possessed any extraordinary skill, except the ability to move quietly through the jungle and the capability of winning a fight. Tynan suspected that he would need them before the mission was over.

Bobbi finished her steak, set her knife and fork down, and said, "You've been very quiet."

Tynan smiled. "Sorry. Been thinking about the mission. Trying to figure out who to take."

"You could invite me," said Bobbi.

"You sure you want to go? Living in the jungle surrounded by who knows what for how long?"

"Don't sugarcoat it that way, Mark. Spit it out. Tell me what it'll really be like."

Tynan was about to say something in response when he realized that she was baiting him. He saw the waiter hovering nearby, wanting to swoop in with the check to get them out of there. He wadded the napkin from his lap and tossed it to the table, signaling that he had finished.

The waiter asked if they wanted desert, and when both declined, he left the check sitting at Tynan's right hand. Bobbi reached across the table and picked it up. She glanced at it and then said, "Embassy is picking this up."

"Fine," said Tynan. "I never turn down free food."

Bobbi added in a tip, signed the check, and then scribbled an account number on the bottom. She waited for Tynan to pull out her chair. At the doorway to the restaurant, she stopped and looked out into the drizzle.

"Let's get a cab," she suggested.

Tynan could see that it wasn't raining that hard. He felt the need to walk, even if he did get wet. He had been through so much during the last twelve hours that he just wanted the freedom that walking through the drizzle would give him.

"Let's not," he said. "It's not raining that hard."

"All right," said Bobbi.

Outside, they hugged the buildings, dodging along under awnings and building overhangs where possible, under trees when they were the only shelter available. Tynan put an arm around Bobbi's shoulders for the little protection it would give her.

In a few minutes they were soaked as the sky seemed to open up and the rain came again. For a moment they stood in the shelter of a hotel awning, watching the rain bounce off the street and the colors from the neon seem to fade and run as they were reflected from the wet surfaces.

Finally Bobbi laughed. "Let's go on. I can't get any wetter, and it's turning chilly."

For a moment Tynan looked up the six steps that led into the hotel and wondered if they should just disappear for a couple of hours. Then he thought better of it. He took Bobbi's hand, and together they left the shelter of the awning, trotting down the street. Bobbi began dodging toward the puddles, trying to splash Tynan. In seconds they were both laughing as they swerved to avoid the umbrella-toting pedestrians around them.

They were stopped at the embassy entrance by the Marine guard, who didn't recognize Bobbi right away. He then let them pass, shaking his head as if he disapproved.

"I've got some towels up in my office," said Bobbi. "We can dry off there."

Tynan followed up the wide staircase to the second floor. They walked down a hallway, carpeted in red and lined with paintings of the ambassadors for the last hundred years. Around a corner they came to an elevator. Bobbi used a key to call it and then took them to the fourth floor. They exited into another carpeted hallway, but the carpeting wasn't as plush. It was a worn powder blue. The walls had no paintings, and a couple of the lights were burned out, making it dim.

She unlocked her office, pushed the door open, and reached inside, feeling for the light switch. She then stepped back and let Tynan enter first.

The office was bigger than he had thought it would be. There was a wooden desk set in front of the window so that she could turn in her chair and look at the street below. There were two brown leather wingback chairs. In one corner, near a floor-to-ceiling bookcase, were a couch, two chairs, and a table arranged into a conference area.

"Why don't you sit down," she said as she crossed the floor to the closet, "while I get the towels."

"I don't want to get anything wet."

"Don't worry about it. There's nothing in here that will be ruined by a little water."

She disappeared for a moment and then reappeared with a couple of towels draped over her shoulder. In her hand she held another towel with which she was rubbing her hair. She approached him, kicked off her shoes, and then handed a towel to Tynan.

She finished with her hair and dropped the towel to the floor. When she saw that Tynan was watching her, she reached up under her skirt and peeled her panty hose down over her legs. She took it off and tossed it into the corner. Next she reached behind her, worked the snap there, and then forced down the zipper. She shrugged her shoulders so that the dress fell away. She pushed it over her hips and let it pool around her feet. She did the same thing with her slip, and finally she was standing in front of Tynan wearing only her red bikini panties. Without a word, she picked up her towel and began drying her body.

"That's my job," he said as he watched her drying herself.

She let go of the towel, spread her arms and said, "Well, come on. I haven't got all day."

Tynan moved to her and took the towel from her hand. Carefully he rubbed her shoulders. He let the towel slip until he was massaging her breasts. Tynan dropped to his knees and dried her legs one at a time, kissing her thighs as he did it. He stood again, pulled her to him so that he could get at her back. He let the towel fall to the floor, holding her close. He kissed her neck and could feel her nipples stiffen against him. He eased one hand under the waistband of her panties, feeling her. He pushed at them, forcing them down over her hips.

She began to unbutton his shirt, opening it and pushing it aside. With one hand, she worked his belt and unfastened his pants.

"You're still wet," she said.

"Well, you'll have to do something about that," he said. He stepped back slightly and looked at her. She was naked now, her panties around her ankles. He bent toward her and kissed her between the breasts, one hand squeezing her right nipple gently.

A low moan escaped her lips. "You'll never get dry," she said huskily, "if you don't quit that."

"The air will dry me," he responded.

Bobbi put a hand to his chest to stop him for a moment. "Let me make sure the door is locked."

He watched her as she moved to the door. She turned the lock and stood there for a moment. Then, slowly, she pivoted until she was facing him again. She licked her lips and rubbed a hand down her bare arm. She put her left hand on her stomach, massaging her belly, as she continued to stare into his eyes.

Tynan finished removing his clothes. He moved to her, kissed her throat, her chin, and then her lips. He felt her tongue probing and opened his mouth. Still kissing, he picked her up and carried her to the couch, where he set her down.

She leaned back, pulled him with her, and reached between them. She shifted slightly, drawing him with her, and eased him closer.

"Now," she said. "Right now."

Later, the sweat having dried from them, Tynan rolled over and nearly fell off the couch. He put a hand flat on the floor and then sat up. He looked at Bobbi stretched out beside him and said, "I've got to get back downstairs."

Bobbi sat up and kissed Tynan's shoulder. "Tell you what," she said, smiling. "You hurry through your meeting and I'll wait here. I'll see if I can find something sexy to wear."

Tynan got to his feet, found his shorts, and put them on. He sat in one of the chairs so that he could don his socks. "What could be more sexy than what you're already wearing? Or maybe I should say not wearing."

"I don't know," she said, stretching her legs. "Maybe something tiny in black lace."

"That would do it," said Tynan. He picked up the rest of his clothes and finished dressing rapidly. He ran a hand through his hair, felt the tangle, and asked, "You wouldn't have a comb I could borrow, would you?"

Bobbi got up and went to her desk. She found a comb and held it out for him.

"Thanks. How about a mirror?"

"Closet door."

Tynan combed his hair. He noticed that his clothes were wrinkled, but there was nothing he could do about it now. He handed the comb back and said, "You're going to stay right here, aren't you?"

"I'll be here after the meeting," she said, coming around the desk to face him.

Tynan took her in his arms and kissed her. His hands were on her sides, his thumbs caressing her nipples.

"If you plan to make your meeting, you better stop that."

"Just something to remember me by," said Tynan. He moved to the door and then stopped. "Say, how am I supposed to use the elevator? I don't have a key."

"You don't need one up here. Only on the first and second floor. Just press the button marked B-1 and you'll be down there."

"You're just going to let me go running around the embassy without an escort?"

Bobbi picked up the phone. She pressed a button and said, "You want me to summon one of the Marines?"

"What? Are you suggesting that a Navy officer needs help from a Marine?"

"No."

"Good. Well, I'm going to split now. See you in a couple of hours."

"I'll be here."

Tynan opened the door and stepped into the hallway. He looked back for a second. Bobbi was leaning against her desk, her arms braced on it, her elbows locked. He let his eyes roam from her face down her naked body to her ankles.

"Yeah," he mumbled. "I'll be back."

He walked down the hall, entered the elevator, and took it to the basement. He exited and was stopped by the guard, who checked the access list he had been given and let Tynan through the iron gate. Conway met him in the hall and took him back to the conference room that they had used earlier that day.

Inside, when Tynan was seated, Conway asked, "Are there any questions that you have thought of since we talked last?"

"About a thousand," said Tynan, "but I'll wait until I've been briefed and see if anything comes up."

Conway pointed at the door, and Wheeler, who had been standing by it, out of the way, opened it. A young Air Force staff sergeant entered. She was wearing the standard dress blue uniform of jacket and short skirt. She had blond hair piled on her head, a pale complexion, and bright blue eyes. She looked nervous.

"All right, Sergeant, you may begin when ready."

She nodded and cleared her throat. "Good evening," she said. "I'm Sergeant Rachel Sanders. Tonight's briefing contains some material that is classified as secret. Please do not discuss it with uncleared personnel or outside control areas."

She hesitated as the lights dimmed and the screen descended from the ceiling. A slide showing the continent of Africa appeared, and Sanders grabbed a pointer that was hanging on the lectern that stood in the corner.

"As I understand it," she began, "the crash site is located forty-two miles from the Atlantic Ocean in sub-Saharan Africa just off the Cameroon plateau. The area is heavily jungled, which makes satellite imagery difficult. However, these photos . . ." She paused as Africa dissolved into a black-and-white picture showing the tops of trees, riverbeds, and roads. Bright red SECRET stamps obscured some of the details on the top and bottom of the picture.

"These photos," she repeated, "show the likely crash site. The problem is that the pictures were taken from one hundred three miles, and a crashed airplane no longer resembles an airplane. It is a tangled mass of broken metal and random parts. A detailed description and maps will be supplied at the conclusion of the briefing.''

The photos faded and the lights came on. Sanders moved to the lectern and set her notes on it. "The political situation in the target country isn't all bad," she said. "We're dealing with a country that is not aligned with either the East or the West, but will go to the one that offers the best deal. There is a standing military, the largest in sub-Saharan Africa outside of South Africa and Rhodesia. It is marked by a couple of crack battalions that form a presidential guard; the remainder is poorly trained and ill equipped. They claim a modern Air Force but fly World War II–vintage fighters, some of them from the Third Reich. They have three helicopters, one used for spare parts and the other two at the disposal of the president.

"They have a navy, but it is little more than a coast guard with small patrol boats. They claim territorial waters out about sixty miles but have no way of enforcing that. Realistically, their territorial waters are two to three miles. Patrols are erratic.''

Sanders flipped a page and continued. "The local population is split into more than two hundred tribal groups scattered throughout the country. The major languages are English and French, although there are fifty or more tribal languages and dialects. There are no major roads or highways and no nationwide method of communication. There is a radio station in the capital city that claims the power to broadcast throughout the country, but with so many different languages and dialects, the message probably doesn't reach half the people.

"Local climate ranges from mild to hot and humid. Temperature range is sixty to eighty degrees. There is one season, hot and wet. Rainfall averages sixty inches a year, though from year to year it varies quite a bit, with the low being somewhere around twenty five inches and the high over a hundred inches.

"The political situation is fairly stable, so the major threat will be the local animal life. Nearly half the snakes are poisonous. Some have bites that will do little more than make the victim sick. Others, such as the black mamba, termed the most deadly snake in the world, have a bite that is nearly always fatal, although there are antivenins available."

Tynan interrupted. "Why is the black mamba considered the most deadly snake in the world?"

"Because," said Sanders, glancing up from her notes, "it will attack with no provocation and it will continue to attack. The victims always have multiple wounds from the snake. The rattlesnake, for example, bites once and then retreats. The mamba keeps biting as long as the victim is in range."

"Wonderful," said Tynan. "Just the sort of news I was hoping for."

"Then you'll be glad to know," she said, "that there are scorpions, but they are found mostly in the hot and dry regions. There are driver ants, similar to the army ants of South America, that sweep through the jungle devouring everything in their path. And there is the tsetse fly that lives throughout Africa that can transmit sleeping sickness to humans."

"That's encouraging," said Tynan.

"There is plenty of game, if it becomes necessary to supplement your rations. Antelopes, from the tiny royal antelope no bigger than a rabbit to the giant eland which is as big as an ox, are abundant. Rabbits and hares are plentiful, as are squirrels and monkeys. There are perch and catfish in the rivers. Of course, the jungle is alive with plants that are edible."

Sanders turned over the last of her papers. "That about covers it. Are there any questions?"

"Yes," said Tynan. "Soviet interest?"

Wheeler stepped out of the shadows and said, "There is no Soviet interest right now. Latest check of the airport at the capital showed that no Soviet aircraft have landed in the last two days."

"Water temperature?" asked Tynan.

"Water temperature?" repeated Sanders. "Why would you want to know that?"

"If I'm required to swim ashore, it would be nice to know whether I'll survive the swim or not."

"Ah, yes. Water temperature is fairly high, although there are some cold-water currents in the vicinity. Low range is probably about forty-eight degrees in the worst of conditions."

"You touched on the local military. You have a listing of the distribution?"

"Most of them are in the capital," said Sanders. "At least the crack troops. They are the presidential guard. There are scattered outposts, but these are only haphazardly manned by poorly trained troops. Many of them get fed up and fade into the jungle." She stopped talking and looked expectantly at Tynan, waiting for his next question.

Finally Conway moved to the front and said, "Anything else you need from the sergeant?"

"Nothing that immediately springs to mind."

"All right, Rachel, that will be all. Leave the maps and the photos. We'll need those."

"Yes, sir." She handed him a folder. To Tynan, she said, "Please remember that some of the information covered is classified as secret."

When she was out of the room, Wheeler sat down next to Tynan and opened the folder that Conway handed him. He spread the pictures out, could see nothing on them, and unfolded the map. Someone had marked the crash site on it.

"Okay," said Wheeler. "As you can see, there is nothing around the airplane except jungle. No villages, no roads handy, no large sources of water. Nothing. It is close to the coast, and it shouldn't take you more than two, three days to reach it if you infiltrate from the ocean. Such a route solves a number of logistical problems. Same with exfiltration. So close to the coast it would be mindless to use helicopters. It also may negate your desire for prearranged resupply points. In fact, since it is so close to the coast, a large number of problems are eliminated. All you have to do is get in there and blow up the plane."

"Looks like the crash site is only twenty-five miles from that little town," said Tynan, pointing at the map. "Shows that it has an airport with a paved runway."

"Correct," said Wheeler, "but we don't want to announce that we're going in. That's why we feel the coast provides the perfect infiltration route. Besides, we want this whole thing kept under wraps until we have the plane destroyed. We don't want Redland sending in a team to recover it. The last thing we need is a confrontation with the Soviet Union."

"So you want me and my team to swim in, hike through the jungle, and blow up the plane."

"Exactly. After the plane is destroyed, we'd like you to hike back out and exfiltrate the way you came in. That way no one would be the wiser. A low-profile, quiet mission that no one knows about."

"Yes, sir."

"There is one other thing," said Wheeler. "You will have to take a radio. I know what you said about them, but we can't have you running around a foreign nation without a method of making contact with us if it becomes necessary. You will remain on radio silence until the Blackbird is destroyed and you need to begin the exfiltration. Neither Colonel Conway nor I feel that a single, short message will compromise your mission.''

Tynan thought about protesting, just to find out how much power he had. Instead he conceded the point because it really didn't matter that much. He said, ''Aye, aye, sir.''

''So who and what do you need?''

Tynan rocked back in his chair and reviewed the thoughts he had had since late afternoon. He nodded once and then sat forward. ''Give me some paper. I've a couple of names for you. I know one guy who is a whiz at demolitions, but I don't know if we can get him.''

''You just put it down,'' said Conway. ''We'll take care of getting the people you need.''

For the next thirty minutes, Tynan prepared his list. He included everything that he could think of, even the things that should have been obvious. When he got to the weapons portion, he asked, ''We going in sterile?''

Conway shrugged, but Wheeler said, ''That would probably be best. Why?''

''Weapons. Instead of M-16s, which are in fairly short supply, we can take the equivalent.'' He smiled at a private joke. ''If you have them, AK-47s. That'll make the Soviets happy.''

''You let us worry about finding the stuff. You just put down what you want.''

Tynan nodded and went back to his writing. When he finished, he pushed the list at Wheeler, who picked it up, scanned it, and said, ''Shouldn't be a problem.''

''Great,'' said Tynan, standing. ''Two things you should do. Once you get in touch with Brian Ross—

he's the demolition guy—you cross-check my list of
explosives with him. There might be something that
he'll want that I didn't think of, and if he's going to
be the one destroying the plane, we'll want to keep
him happy.''

"Makes sense," said Wheeler. "And the other?"

"Jones is in Scotland on that SAS training mission
you pulled me from. See if you can't arrange to send
the same plane for him under the same circumstances.
Along with the same stewardess.''

Wheeler made a quick note and then asked, "He's
an enlisted man?"

"Yeah, but that shouldn't make a difference. I want
him for the mission, and he deserves the ride. Pretend
he's an admiral's kid or something.''

"All right," said Wheeler. "We'll see what we can
do. Now, where will you be?''

"I've got a late date with Bobbi Harris. I don't
know what she has in mind.''

"Just leave us a number where we can reach you,"
said Conway. "We've got to hurry because we don't
want someone else finding the plane.''

"Right," said Tynan, thinking that earlier in the
day he had heard people saying that they had to hurry,
but no one could say why. It seemed to have come
full circle. "Right," he repeated. "We have to
hurry.''

6

The morning dawned bright and cloudless, and if it hadn't been for the pools of muddy water standing on the ramp area and in the tiny parking lot, Molodin wouldn't have known that it had rained the night before. He stood just outside the terminal building, looking at the sun burning through a bright blue sky and into the deep green of the jungle. Around him was a silence that he never heard in the city or even the country areas near his home in Moscow. He could hear the quiet buzz of insects, and the chatter of the monkeys as they screamed at one another, but nothing that suggested civilization.

The sky overhead was cloudless and the humidity seemed to hang in the air like yesterday's wet laundry. Molodin felt the sweat bead on his forehead as he tried to breathe and trickle down his back as he moved.

"The men are assembled," said Krothov, approaching from the terminal.

"And?" said Molodin, turning to look at his executive officer. The tall man's uniform, a dull green, was already soaked, large ragged stains under the arms and down the front, looking almost as if he had run through the rain shower the night before.

"They are waiting for instructions." Krothov smiled. "It was difficult to convince the scientists and engineers that they had to rise early."

Molodin smiled at the image of his men trying to convince the civilians that they had to get out of bed, even though the beds were sleeping bags on air mattresses on the upper level of the terminal building. He asked, "Has everyone eaten breakfast?"

"We have been waiting for instructions."

"Fine. You have them. Make sure that everyone has a good breakfast. I want all our men to use a great deal of salt on their food because of the high temperatures and high humidity here."

"Yes, Comrade."

"Have you seen our local contact?"

"Yes, sir," said Krothov.

"Good. Do you know his name?"

"He told it to me, but it was something that was nearly impossible to pronounce. He did say that he was an elevated major. I don't know what kind of rank that is, so I have addressed him as only major."

"That is nice to know. I shall talk to him and see what he has learned during the night."

Krothov pointed back to the terminal. "Saw him wandering around in there a little while ago. Had a couple of his friends with him."

"I shall talk to him," said Molodin. "You have your instructions."

"Yes, sir." Krothov looked up at the sun and wiped a sleeve across his sweat-damp forehead. He turned and headed back to the terminal.

The local major appeared before Molodin could move. He said, in English, "Good morning. I trust you slept well."

Molodin ignored that and asked in French, "Did you locate the plane?"

"I am afraid that we have failed to pinpoint the location," said the major.

"But you have something?"

"Let us go inside where it is cooler and we can sit down. I will have coffee brought. Or tea, if you prefer."

"Yes, that would be pleasant."

Inside, using the office they had the day before, the major spread a map of the surrounding territory out on the desk. He pointed to it and said, "Yesterday you told us that you believed the plane had crashed in this vicinity some forty kilometers south of here."

"That is correct," agreed Molodin.

"There are stories," said the major. "Stories of a machine from the sky that smashed into the ground, but no one seems to know exactly where. They all point away from their villages, in the same general direction, but no one has actually seen it. Rumors. Stories. That is all that I have." He waved a hand in the air.

"Let me ask you this," said Molodin. "Is there an easy way to get into that general location? Are there roads? Could we fly in if we had the proper equipment?"

"There are few roads through the jungle. There is one, however, that we can use, but from there the search must continue on foot."

"You said 'we'. How many men are you planning to use in the search?" asked Molodin.

"I have two hundred standing by."

"Then we shall begin the search as soon as my men have finished eating their breakfast."

Tynan woke up sore. His body ached from his toes to the top of his head. He felt like he had been run over by a steamroller and the driver had backed up to see if he really had hit someone. Tynan didn't know if it was from all the activity with Bobbi, or if it was because of the SAS exercise, or a combination of both. He decided that he didn't care. He just lay there, on his back, staring at the white ceiling, wondering if he would ever move again.

A moment later he heard the door open and turned his head. Bobbi entered, carrying a white tray that was piled high with food. She was wearing a black, hip-length lace robe that had a single silk bow fastening it at the throat and that concealed nothing. She was naked from the hips down.

"You dress like that," said Tynan, "and somebody is going to knock that food out of your hands."

She set the tray carefully on the edge of the bed, next to Tynan, and then sat down beside it. "Yeah," she said, "them and whose army?"

Tynan reached over and plucked a slice of toast from one of the stacks. He bit into it, chewed, and then asked, "What the hell time is it?"

"Little before eight. You've got time to eat, grab a shower before the big meet."

"You talk to anyone at the embassy this morning?" asked Tynan. He reached over and rubbed her shoulder.

"Briefly. Said that your friend Jones arrived about five. Couple of others, Boone and Sterne, will be in before nine. They couldn't find Ross, so they've called in another guy named, ah, Hollinger. Lee Hollinger."

"You know anything about him?" asked Tynan. "I knew a Hollinger a couple of years back. Big, burly guy with dark hair and bad sinuses. Called him Animal because he liked blowing things up."

Bobbi pushed her hair out of the way so that she could look at Tynan out of the corner of her eye. "File didn't say anything about him except that he was an expert on demolitions. They're still trying to find Ross, but they weren't taking any chances.''

"It wouldn't hurt to have both of them on the mission.''

"You know," said Harris, moving closer, "that, if you skip breakfast, we still have time for some fun.''

Tynan decided, as he walked down the corridor in the embassy, that he hadn't minded skipping breakfast. He entered the conference room that they had used the night before and found Jones sitting there talking to Wheeler.

When Tynan entered, Jones got to his feet, grinned, and said, "Thanks for the plane ride, Lieutenant. It was great and beat the hell out of eating insects during a freezing night in Scotland.''

Wheeler interrupted. "We've got another flight to catch. The rest of your people are assembling at Southampton, where a ship is waiting for you.''

"Did you get Ross or Hollinger?" asked Tynan.

"Both," said Wheeler. He moved to the door and opened it. "We've transportation waiting upstairs for you.''

"Then let's go," said Tynan. On the way up, he realized that he wouldn't have a chance to say good-bye to Bobbi and hoped that she would understand. She should, given all the circumstances. She knew the score.

They were taken to the limousine that had the blue embassy pennant flying from the front fender. Wheeler opened the door and let Tynan and Jones get into the back. Before he shut the door, he said, "The driver will get you to the airport and onto the plane. Someone should meet you at the other end.''

Tynan nodded his understanding and sat back in the deep seats. When the door shut and the engine started, a deep, quiet rumbling that could barely be heard inside the car, Tynan reached out and grabbed the knobs of the built-in equipment. He found a bar, stocked with several brands of bourbon and scotch and a variety of mixers. There was a small television concealed by another door, and a bank of telephones hidden behind a third.

"Drink up," said Tynan. "We'll probably have little opportunity in the next few weeks."

"That's all right, sir," said Jones. He pulled a Hershey bar from one of his pockets. His body heat had softened the chocolate.

"Suit yourself."

They reached the airport thirty minutes later. It was not Heathrow, London's international airport, but a military field where a twin-engine jet like the one he had used yesterday stood by. They were hustled through the flight operations, escorted out the door, and told to climb the steps. Inside the aircraft, an American Air Force major told them to buckle in and then disappeared up front.

Moments later they were airborne, climbing high above London. Out the cabin window Tynan could see the silver ribbon of the Thames that bisected the city. To the east he could see the shimmering of the English Channel. Then he sat back, closed his eyes, and wondered just how in the hell Bobbi had managed to get from the embassy in Saigon to the embassy in London. Not that it mattered. He had been glad to see her, and they certainly had had fun the night before.

It seemed that only minutes had passed since take-off, but they were already descending, making the approach to the local base. As the plane rolled to a halt Tynan could see a staff car waiting on the ramp.

The plume of exhaust told him that the engine was running.

They were hurried from the plane to the car and were on the road almost before the aircraft rolled to a stop. It didn't take long to get to the port facilities. They drove out on the pier, stopping fifty feet from the gangplank of the ship. They were told to board, and to hurry because the captain had been waiting for them.

The officer of the deck met them at the gangplank and gave them permission to board. He escorted them forward, along a companionway, to the wardroom. He opened the hatch and said, ''Your men are assembled inside.''

Tynan stepped in and surveyed the room. The four men sat there reading calmly. Ross held a clipboard that might have contained a list of the equipment.

''Well,'' said Tynan, ''let's get started.''

As Tynan spoke to his team the ship weighed anchor and began manuevering to leave port.

The major had arranged for the trucks to pick them up at the terminal building. Molodin had divided his men into two teams, one to be commanded by Lieutenant Krothov and the other by himself. Each of the teams would work with four teams of the natives. The major would operate as a liaison among all the teams, coordinating the activities from a point three or four kilometers behind the others.

The trucks were old American-made Fords that roared with age and strain. They bumped along the jungle roads, paths actually, with the broad leaves of the palms scraping at the canvas covers stretched over the backs. Molodin instinctively ducked as branches of the trees hit the cracked windshield of the truck's cab.

Molodin's truck rolled to a halt at a wide place where the jungle had been cut back, letting them get off the road. Molodin opened the door and got out. He waited while the men in the back dropped to the ground. One of them remained in the truck, handing down the equipment, the knapsacks and weapons.

When the men were ready, Molodin consulted his map, the search grids already marked out on it. One of the black men from the major's company studied the map too. He pointed to the jungle and spoke in English.

Molodin pretended that he didn't understand him and said, "You must speak French."

The man shrugged and said, in English, "I do not know French."

For a moment Molodin didn't say a word. Finally, in English, he said, "You will be the point. You will lead in that direction."

The man nodded and entered the jungle. Molodin watched his men spread out, forming a normal military patrol. Pankovski fell in as slack. Kudira hesitated, taking up the rearguard position while the remainder of the men strung out along the path.

Travel near the road was easy. The jungle was thin, with little ground cover. They moved rapidly, pushing away the branches of the bushes that got in the way, hacking at others with machetes. Since it wasn't a military patrol, they didn't have to worry about noise discipline or leaving signs that others might spot. They joked with each other as they cut their way deeper into the trees.

Overhead, the sun baked them. Within seconds of leaving the trucks, the men felt the strength draining from them in the humidity and heat of the late morning. Molodin stopped them frequently to drink from the canteens they carried, cautioning them not to drink the water too rapidly because it would make them sick.

He found that he had to halt them often, giving them five- and ten-minute breaks every twenty or thirty minutes. None of them other than the natives were used to the heat that seemed to surround them, nearly crushing them, making their movements sluggish. And even the frequent breaks did little to alleviate the problem. The men dragged themselves to their feet, stumbling forward, their heads down, watching the trail directly in front of them.

Several times Molodin had told them they were supposed to be searching for a plane, not just strolling through the jungle. They must keep their eyes open, their heads swiveling from side to side, looking for clues. A piece of metal, a scrap of cloth, anything that didn't belong in the jungle.

At noon they halted, Molodin furious at the enforced snail's pace. They had hiked little more than a kilometer or two from where they had left the trucks. At this rate, the plane would rust into nothing before they could find it. But he knew that he couldn't require the men to walk faster or search harder. He hadn't expected the humidity to take the toll that it did. The terrain, though rather flat, did not make travel any easier. It was rapidly becoming a test of endurance. Good training, if that was all it was supposed to be. But they had to find the plane before the Americans began searching for it.

For an hour Molodin sat quietly in the shade of a giant palm tree. He ate his noon ration slowly, watching the others. As soon as they had finished eating, most slumped over to nap. They unbuttoned their uniform shirts, but there was no breeze stirring. They unbuckled their equipment, setting it aside. A few fanned themselves, the sweat running down their faces, staining their clothes, and soaking their skins.

In a combat environment, Molodin would never have let the men get as sloppy as they had become, but it wasn't combat and it was too hot to fight about. He had, in fact, unbuttoned his own shirt for the little cooling it offered.

At the end of an hour, Molodin got to his feet and told his men it was time to move out. They grumbled to themselves, not one of them saying anything loud enough for Molodin to overhear. He couldn't blame them, however. The last thing he wanted to do was get to his feet and begin the march again.

"We must make use of the time we have," he told them as they formed into the search party. "The Americans are not going to sit idly by and let us have their secret airplane. The Americans will be coming soon, and when they arrive, I would like them to find empty ground where their plane crashed."

7

The ship drifted silently just over three miles off the African coast. The sun had disappeared an hour earlier, but the heat of the tropics had remained. Tynan stood on the fantail and watched as the crew circulated. Those on the outboard side smoked in the gentle breeze, the glowing tips of their cigarettes invisible to anyone on the coast because they were facing out to sea.

Tynan studied the darkened coast. He could see an occasional light in the distance bobbing through the jungle, maybe the headlamp of a truck or the lantern of a farmer returning late from his fields. Far to the north, against the black of the landscape, he could see the glow of the only large city in the vicinity. He knew that the electrical power was supposed to stay on all night in the city, but that the generators there often failed.

Jones approached from the port side of the darkened ship. He stood near Tynan for a moment, staring into the night, and then reported, in a quiet voice, "All set, Skipper."

Tynan looked down into the blackness of the ocean with its streams of phosphorescence barely visible. He didn't relish the three-mile swim, but it beat jumping out of an airplane at twenty-five or thirty thousand feet to free-fall to fifteen hundred and then land at night in the jungle where he could easily break an arm or leg or even his back.

"Okay, get on back to the men and tell them I'll be down in a minute or two. Ross and Hollinger complete their inventory of the explosives?"

"Yes, sir," said Jones. "Ross claimed he could blow up a battleship with what the CIA had gotten for him."

"About forty minutes, then," said Tynan.

Jones knew that meant the swim would begin in about forty minutes. He nodded and said, "Aye, aye, sir."

Tynan took one last look at the country. There wasn't much that he could see now that it was night. There was a small beach, lined with dark sand, that led directly into the jungle. Forty or fifty miles inland, almost due east, was the wreck of the SR-71. Tynan just couldn't see how that was going to be a problem. No one knew they were coming, no one was expecting them, and they weren't there to destroy anything other than the wreckage of the plane. It should have been a piece of cake. Tynan wondered why he was so worried about it.

He turned and headed for the hatch that would take him into the wardroom where he had set up his temporary staging area. It was the only place on the ship that had the necessary deck space and the limited access that Tynan demanded. All the ship's officers had finished their evening meal, so there wasn't a conflict with them.

He hesitated at the hatch. He wiped the sweat from his face and tried to put on a calm look. His insides were churning, just like before a combat assignment in Vietnam. He tried to tell himself again that the mission was a piece of cake, a training mission that would give him some valuable experience in a jungle other than that of Southeast Asia, and that there was no real danger, other than some of the nasty local fauna. Still, he was worried, but he didn't want to communicate that anxiety to the men.

He opened the hatch. Jones was sitting at the head of a table covered with a clean white cloth, twisting the dials of the radio he had been given by the CIA man in London. This was not a PRC-25 like the ones he was used to in Vietnam. This was a bulkier radio with a long whip antenna that was supposed to have the range to reach the ship even after Tynan and his men reached the crash site and the ship was ten or twelve miles off the African coast.

Hollinger sat on the floor, packages of explosives scattered around him as he checked them. He was taking the inventory that Jones had reported completed. As usual, his uniform looked as if it had been slept in and none of the pockets were buttoned. There were smudges of grease and dirt on his shirt. He hadn't shaved in two days. Tynan didn't like spit-and-polish sailors, believing that they sometimes sacrificed specialized job skills for military talents that had little practical value, but Hollinger seemed to have taken it too far in the other direction. He was living up to his nickname of Animal.

Ross sat next to him. Ross seemed to be the opposite of Hollinger. His uniform was neatly pressed, the pockets buttoned. His dark hair was combed, and he had polished his boots to a high gloss recently.

Tynan moved closer to them and said, ''What's the captain say about all these explosives in here?''

''We told him that there was no danger as long as we didn't have the det cord or detonators near them. He didn't seem real happy about it, but he didn't say anything else.''

"I thought you had finished the inventory."

"We did. We're just trying to split the stuff up into small groups so that we can pack it in. One guy is going to get to carry the det cord and one guy the detonators, while the rest of us carry the explosives."

"Great!" said Jones. "Just what I want to do. Swim to shore carrying a bunch of explosives."

Tynan ignored the remark and glanced at Sterne, who was sitting on the broken-down settee reading a tattered copy of *Penthouse*. His weapon, a captured Chicom AK-47, was set beside him. At his feet was his knapsack. His web gear and pistol belt were on the settee next to him. He didn't seem to be worried about anything.

Sitting alone in a corner was Boone. He had his combat knife out and was slowly stropping it, although it already had a razor-sharp edge. He was paying no attention to any of the others in the wardroom.

Tynan pulled out one of the chairs at the table and sat down. He studied his men for a moment, but before he could speak there was a tapping at the hatch. He turned to see one of the ship's officers standing there.

"Yes?"

"Ah, Lieutenant Tynan," said the officer, "we just got this in. Message from your Mr. Wheeler in London."

Tynan held out a hand, wiggled his fingers, and said, "Give it here."

The officer handed it over and then said, "I'll wait for a response, if you care to make one."

Tynan unfolded the paper, scanned the contents, and then read it carefully. There wasn't much to it. Two paragraphs providing him with new information. When he finished, he said, "I have no response."

Without a word the officer left. Sterne looked up from his magazine and said, "What's that all about?"

"New information," answered Tynan without looking up. "Seems that our CIA friends didn't cover all the bases. They checked on the capital's international airport, figuring that the Soviets would use it if they planned to put a team into the area. Now they've checked the other major airport and identified an AN-22 Cock on the ground. It has been there for, at a minimum, twenty-four hours."

"Which means?" asked Sterne.

"Which means that we can expect that there are Soviets looking for the Blackbird."

"How many people does the Cock carry?" asked Jones with a grin.

Hollinger looked up from his pile of explosives and said, "It's a transport. I would imagine that it holds thirty, forty, maybe more."

"And how in the hell would you know that?" asked Sterne.

"By the name," said Hollinger. "The Soviet designation is AN, but the NATO identification is Cock. Starts with a *C,* which means it's a cargo plane. NATO designates the fighters with words that begin with an *F* and bombers with *B*'s."

"Thanks for the information. That's something I've always wanted to know," said Sterne sarcastically.

"Boone," said Tynan, "why don't you see if you can find the intelligence officer and see what he can tell us about the Soviet plane. Nothing detailed, just how many people it will carry, the range, and things like that."

Boone slipped his knife back into the scabbard and stood. He glanced at his equipment as if wondering if it would be safe to leave it and then shrugged. He moved to the hatch and disappeared through it.

"Is there anything else that they forgot to mention?" asked Sterne.

Tynan glanced idly at the message and said, "That seems to be the latest. Still shouldn't affect our mission."

"Oh no," said Sterne. "Not at all. Soviets running all over the place shouldn't bother us. Except they seem to be operating aboveboard and we're about to sneak into the country. They'll have local help and we'll have none."

"They don't know where the plane crashed," said Jones. "We do."

"They must know something since they picked the airport closest to the crash site," said Tynan quietly. He thought for a moment and then said, "Of course, there might be other reasons they landed there. They might not even know that a Blackbird is down."

"Do you really believe that?" asked Sterne.

"No. Not at all," said Tynan.

Boone reappeared at that moment. "Intel officer said that there wasn't much interesting to tell us about the Cock." He glanced at his notes. "He just opened a copy of *Jane's All the World's Aircraft* and wrote this down. He said that there were permanent seats behind the flight deck on the upper level for about thirty people but that the lower areas used for cargo could carry troops if necessary. It is the second-largest cargo plane in the world, ranking after the C-5 which can carry three hundred and fifty troops."

"Christ," said Sterne. "They could have a fucking battalion on the ground."

Suddenly Tynan had a direction for the anxiety. It all made sense now. The CIA had said that they didn't want to use their own operatives because they didn't want to alert the Soviets to the importance of the downed plane. It meant that the CIA had expected the Soviets to try to recover it. It meant that the CIA had known that the Soviets would try. They just hadn't bothered telling Tynan. At least they had had the courtesy to tell him when they found evidence of Soviet presence.

Still, the whole deal was on a low level. The Soviets sneaking into a backwater airport meant they didn't want the CIA to know what they were doing. So, rather than bring in the battalion that Sterne was worried about, they had probably sent in a smaller unit, maybe as small as a platoon.

"I would think," said Tynan, "that we could get in and out without having to even see the Soviets. There's a lot of territory to cover, so the odds of us running into them are rather remote."

"And if we do?" asked Sterne pointedly.

"We play it by ear."

"And what does that mean?" asked Sterne.

"It means we play it by ear," snapped Tynan. "It means that we try to avoid all contact with the Soviets. The last thing we need to do is cause some sort of an international incident."

"That doesn't answer the question," said Sterne, his voice rising.

Tynan stared at him for a moment and then glanced toward Hollinger. "Animal, get your stuff packed and ready. I want to be off this ship in less than half an hour."

"Why the sudden rush, Lieutenant?" asked Sterne.

"Because, you fucking idiot, the Soviets are in the area. We must destroy the plane before the Soviets locate it. Get your gear packed in the watertight bags. I want everyone changed into the wet suits in twenty minutes."

"Why the wet suits?" asked Jones. "Water's not that cold."

"I don't want a bunch of white-skinned men trying to sneak ashore tonight. The beach sand is dark. Once we're into the jungle we'll change into camouflaged fatigues.''

Within half an hour, Tynan stood near the cargo net hung over the side of the ship facing away from the beach. Below him in the water was a black two-man rubber raft, and sitting on the side of it were two of his men. Another two stood on the deck with him, lowering the remainder of the equipment, including the explosives that were wrapped in waterproof plastic, over the side.

He watched as Sterne reached up to guide the last of the explosives into the raft. He unfastened the line from them and let Jones haul it back to the deck.

''That's it, Skipper. Everything is on board.''

Tynan turned toward the ship's officer. He was little more than a black shape standing nearby. Tynan grinned and saluted. ''Permission to go ashore.''

The man snapped to attention and returned the salute. ''Permission granted,'' he said formally. ''Good luck. We'll be at the rendezvous point in sev-enty-two hours.''

''Thanks,'' said Tynan. He touched Jones on the back and watched him climb down the net. Tynan swung a leg over, paused, studying the ship for a few seconds. Then he scrambled down, watched the raft rock in the gentle swell of the sea, and timed it so that he could step into it before it dropped into a trough.

As Tynan stepped into the raft the men, Sterne and Hollinger, who had been sitting on the side slipped into the water. Boone and Jones were already in, each holding on to a line on the raft. Tynan untied the line that held the raft against the cargo net. He pushed off then, and when the raft was clear of the ship, Tynan fell into the water.

Slowly, quietly, some of them pushing and some of them pulling the raft, they swam around the stern of the ship. They then turned so that they were swimming toward the shore, just over three miles away. They took it easy, drifting northward with the current, letting the ocean guide them. Periodically one of them would grab the raft, holding it and resting, while the others continued to swim.

As they approached the beach they could hear the surf crashing on it. Soon they didn't have to swim, just hold on to the raft as the breakers dragged them along. In minutes they could stand in the water. Tynan grabbed the line and pulled the raft forward until it was sitting on the sand, the water gently rocking the rear of it.

"Get the equipment to the trees. Let's move it."

Ross grabbed a bundle and started up the beach, running slowly, digging his feet into the loose, dark sand. He hit firmer ground, increased his speed, angling for a slight gap in the vegetation ahead of him. Suddenly he seemed to straighten up and bounce backward, sprawling to the ground, the equipment he had been carrying thrown into the air.

Tynan dropped the line he had been holding. To the others he whispered, "Wait here." He took off, running up the beach. He heard Ross cursing quietly.

"Son of a fucking bitch! Who the fuck put a fucking fence in the fucking way?"

Tynan reached him and knelt beside him. "You okay? What happened?"

"Ran into a fucking fence. Right into it. Hidden in the bushes and trees. Didn't see it."

"Are you all right?"

Ross ran a hand down his chest to his stomach, feeling himself. He found a couple of flaps of rubberized material where the wet suit had torn. He dabbed at them gingerly and held his fingers close to his face, as if looking for blood.

"I'm fine," he said. "Cut myself up a little."

"Hope you had a tetanus shot before you left on the mission," said Tynan.

Ross climbed to his feet and reached down for the bundle he had been carrying. He straightened up, as if trying to recover his dignity, and said, "I'm fine, Skipper."

"Be a little more careful."

"Aye, aye. But you didn't warn us about a fence along the beach."

"Maybe I thought you would be smart enough to know that there would be one in the way."

"Or maybe you didn't know," responded Ross.

"Maybe. I'll help the others with the rest of the equipment while you look around for a way over the fence that won't leave too many signs that we were here."

"Aye, aye, sir."

"And let's cut that 'sir' crap in the field, shall we. No reason to tell anyone who the officers are if we don't have to." Tynan didn't wait for an answer but headed back down the beach to where the others had unloaded the raft.

"You want to sink it or carry it inland?" asked Jones.

"Let's puncture it and take it with us. We'll bury it at the first opportunity." He stopped talking and looked back at the trees where he could just see Ross's silhouette hunting for a place to climb the fence. It hadn't been electrified—Ross hadn't received an electrical shock—but there could be sensors on it. Tynan wondered about that for a moment and then decided against it. The country was too primitive to have anything as sophisticated as electronic sensors on a fence so far from a populated area.

Still, he couldn't shake the idea. He leaned close to Jones and said, "I want you to check out the fence. See if there is an alarm system or sensors along it. Just a quick look. I doubt that they'll have anything, but if they do, it'll be fairly easy to spot."

Jones shouldered his equipment, grabbed the radio in one hand and his weapon, still wrapped in waterproof plastic, and started toward the fence.

Tynan watched him until he dropped his gear just short of the jungle. Jones crouched, studied something, and then crawled along the edge of the beach.

With Hollinger and Sterne, Tynan gathered the rest of the equipment. They carried it to the edge of the jungle and set it there. Hollinger went back for the raft. He used his knife to deflate it, rolled it into a ball, and carried it back up the beach.

"I've got the perfect place to cross the fence," Ross reported a couple of minutes later. "There's a big gap in the wire about fifty yards south of here."

"Okay. Get the equipment down there. I'll go get Jones and meet you there."

He located Jones, who was examining one of the fence posts. "You find anything?" he asked.

"Nope," he answered, standing. "I think it's just an ordinary fence."

"Ross found a gap in it. We'll head down that way."

It didn't take them long to get through the barbed-wire fence and into the jungle. Behind the gap was a narrow path that indicated others had used the same infiltration route, although Tynan suspected it was just natives using the easy access to the beach, maybe for late-night fishing or maybe just for a little late-afternoon swimming. They filtered deeper into the thin jungle vegetation, veered from the path, and began scouting for a concealed campsite. Tynan had decided that they would have to wait near the beach until morning. He wanted to make sure that they had left nothing behind that would tip the authorities to their presence. They would rest through the night and begin the hike in the morning. They would stay clear of the trails and paths, unless they looked as if they hadn't been used for a long while.

Waiting until morning would also give him the chance to check the immediate surroundings and make sure they were in the right spot. He didn't want to spend the night walking the wrong way because he had mistaken a landmark in the dark. All things being equal, he figured to be at the crash site by late the next day.

He held up a hand when he found what he wanted: a place with a source of water and good cover. He had the men change into their camouflaged fatigues, bury the wet suits and the remains of the raft, and then set up a rotating guard for the remainder of the night so that each of them could get some rest. Tynan didn't know when they would have the opportunity again.

"Tomorrow we begin for real," he said. He still worried about the uneasy feeling he had, but he ignored it just as he had for the last several hours.

8

After an entire day of fruitless searching, marked by interrogations of natives who could not comprehend the concept of a gigantic metallic object falling from the sky, Molodin had had enough. He didn't want to rely on the major with his company of ill-trained, brutal louts who seemed more interested in beating the villagers than in extracting information from them. He was tired of the jungle, of the heat, of the humidity. He was sick of the huge insects that buzzed around and of the tiny ones that sucked blood. He was tired of the whole mission and tired of having to answer periodic radio questions from the scientists left at the airport. All in all, it had not been a good day.

Molodin sat in the cab of his truck, his right foot propped on the dashboard, his elbow on his knee. He held a cigarette in his hand, letting it burn down because he wasn't interested in smoking it.

He tried to figure out what had gone wrong. It had been a wasted day. They had walked through the jungle, avoiding the thickets, the streams, and one huge cliff. They had found nothing during their search. No sign of the American plane. No bits of wreckage that would lead to it. No people who had seen it, or pieces of it. Nothing.

He had endured the heat, sweating heavily until his uniform was soaked through. He had downed the water in his canteen quickly and then been forced to drink from the streams they had come to. At first he had avoided it, figuring he would wait until they got back to the airport, but by midafternoon he had been too thirsty to wait. He had filled his canteen but had been nervous about drinking the water.

What he needed to do was find a faster way to search. He flipped his cigarette out the window and pulled a map from his jacket pocket. As near as he could figure, they had searched about forty square kilometers. That was a lot of territory, but there was so much more to search that it could take months to find anything.

He needed aircraft. He needed the helicopters. He would have to talk to the major about it as soon as he could. There was just too much territory for men to search on foot.

Tynan was awake at dawn. He thought about detailing one of the men to go back to the beach but decided to let them sleep. He slipped out of his cover, waved to Ross, who was standing guard fifteen feet away, hidden inside a large bush, and headed west. He followed the game trail to the fence. He crouched there and waited for the sun to climb higher. It hadn't been that long ago that he had been sitting on the wet grass in Scotland, staring at a barn, waiting for the sun to climb higher there.

The shadows on the dark sand of the beach retreated as the surf seemed to chase them. He watched as the land in front of him brightened. He could see footprints in the sand that led from the water's edge to the fence and then along it, to the gap in it. His men had left nothing that would identify them as the people who made the trail.

Tynan stood and turned to head back to the camp. Once there, he woke everyone and told them to eat breakfast. Tynan sat in the shade of a large palm tree, his back against the trunk, and took one of the C-ration meals from his pack. The main course was scrambled eggs and chopped ham. Cold, they were terrible, but Tynan didn't feel like going through the hassle of heating them. In Vietnam they would have used a small chunk of C-4 explosive to heat the rations. The C-4 burned with a hot flame. The only thing was that you couldn't stamp it out because it would explode. But Tynan had no C-4, and the wood available was too damp to burn easily. So, because of all that, Tynan ate the damned things cold, forcing himself to eat because he would need the energy later in the day.

When he finished eating, he gathered up the empty cans and cardboard box, throwing them into the trash pile his men had created. After the trash and the remains of the food had been buried, Tynan sent Sterne out as point and had Hollinger drop off as a rear guard. They moved out into the jungle, heading almost due east, toward the crash site.

Travel through the jungle was easy, compared to what it had been in Vietnam. There were no booby traps to search for. There were no VC lying in ambush to kill them. There were just the dangers of a jungle, the clinging vines to chop through, the undergrowth to fight through, and the constant threat of rain.

Tynan kept the pace slow even though he knew the Russians were probably out searching for the plane too. But the heat and humidity could sap the strength from the strongest men in a matter of hours. Tynan wasn't too worried about Sterne, Jones, or Boone, because each had been in Vietnam until recently, but neither Hollinger nor Ross had been there. They were essential to the mission, and Tynan couldn't take the chance that they would fold up.

The first hour went fine. Within minutes, each of them had been covered with sweat. There was no breeze on the ground, although Tynan swore he could hear the wind rattling the palms and coconuts above them. After the hour, Tynan called a halt. He moved among the men, studying them, looking for the early signs of heat exhaustion. Hollinger was sitting propped against a tree, his face covered with sweat. He was breathing heavily, and his skin was pale. If he hadn't been sweating, Tynan would have been worried. Ross seemed to be in better shape. He was joking quietly with Jones.

They began the patrol again in twenty minutes. Sterne took the point, weaving among the trees, trying to avoid obstacles that would halt them or turn them. He moved carefully, applying the tricks that he had learned in Vietnam. In front of him, he heard something and went to one knee.

Tynan caught him a moment later. He crouched next to Sterne and asked, ''What is it?''

''I heard voices up ahead. I didn't want to move on until I had alerted you.''

Tynan wiped the back of his hand across his lips. ''All right. You and Boone check it out. Leave your packs here. If there is someone in front of us, don't let them hear you.''

''Aye, aye,'' said Sterne.

Tynan worked his way back and told Boone to go with Sterne. He then told the others to get out of sight. They fell off the game trail into the trees, each finding a position that wasn't visible from the trail.

Tynan didn't like the waiting. He had wanted to accompany Sterne but knew that he couldn't. Sterne knew his job, and Tynan had to let him do it. One of the first things he had discovered after he had received his commission was that he couldn't do everything himself. He had to rely on his subordinates to do their jobs.

Ten minutes later, Sterne was back. He leaned close to Tynan so that he could whisper to him.

"There's fifteen men in front of us. Looks like some kind of local militia. Mismatched uniforms, a variety of old, obsolete weapons, and very little discipline. They're eating a meal now. Cooking it in one of those pots you see in the cartoons with a missionary in it, except that it's a lot smaller."

"They have any kind of guard posted?"

"I didn't see anything. All of them are crowded around the pot, waiting to eat."

Tynan sighed. "Can we get around them?"

"I wouldn't think that it would be a major problem," said Sterne. "They're more interested in their lunch than anything else."

"Okay," said Tynan, glancing at his watch. "Take five, and then get ready to move."

It wasn't hard to avoid the local soldiers. Sterne detoured to the north for several hundred meters, turned to the east for another couple of hundred meters, and then went back to the original trail, so that he had circled their position. He kept the pace steady, looking back frequently to make sure that the others were staying near him.

After another hour of fighting through the jungle, Hollinger rushed forward. He tapped Tynan on the shoulder and said, "I think we're being followed."

"What makes you think that?"

"Noise behind us. I can hear them walking along, stumbling over the bushes, crunching twigs, and occasionally hear their voices. I waited for a moment, listening carefully to them. I don't think they know we're here. I think they believe they're all alone in the jungle. It sounds like they just happen to be on the same path as us."

Tynan nodded. "I'll have Sterne change direction. Veer a little bit to the south."

"Aye, aye, sir."

Tynan caught Sterne, who had halted. He was staring into the jungle and said, "I've spotted someone in front of us."

"What the hell is this? Hollinger just reported that the group we bypassed is now on our trail. You've got more in front of us?"

Sterne used the barrel of his rifle to push back one of the branches. In the distance Tynan could see five men. They were squatting around a small fire. Each wore a khaki uniform with a black belt. Two wore peaked caps with black bills, while the other three wore soft caps. The men were all very black, their skin color bordering on ebony. One of them used a long thin stick to stir the fire. Their weapons were leaning against a log near them.

From behind him Tynan heard a burst of laughter. It meant that the first group was closing in on them. He shot a look at the jungle there and then turned his attention back to the group in front.

"Skipper, what'll we do?"

"Get out of sight and let the two groups run into each other. We've got to hide."

At that moment there was a single shot. Both Tynan and Sterne collapsed to the ground, facing forward, then looking back again, but unable to see anything but the jungle vegetation and a single monkey clambering up a tree. Tynan slowly turned so that he was facing the front. The men there had scrambled away from the flames, and the stack of weapons had disappeared. In the trees near the fire he could still see two of the men, but the others had vanished.

"Shit," he said. "That tears it."

"Who fired?" asked Sterne.

"How the fuck do I know? It didn't sound like one of our weapons. Right now I think we're still in the clear."

Then, almost to make a liar of him, there was a burst from one of the AK-47s. Tynan recognized the sound, having heard it so frequently in Vietnam.

That was answered by more shooting, some of it single shot that sounded like a heavy-caliber weapon. Then, from the men who had been gathered by the fire, there was more shooting, but it was poorly aimed. Tynan heard the rounds passing overhead, sounding like angry insects burrowing through the giant palm leaves. He remembered reading or hearing that Africans tended to aim high when shooting. But that didn't make much difference; most men in a firefight tended to aim high.

"Do we shoot back?" asked Sterne.

When Tynan failed to answer the question, Sterne asked it again, this time with a hard edge to his voice that demanded acknowledgment.

"Let's just try to get the fuck out of here," said Tynan breathlessly, as if he had just run a long distance to answer the question. "If we can fade away, maybe the two groups will think they were shooting at each other and won't know that we were in the middle."

Jones appeared then, crawling across the ground, his elbows stained by the soft brown earth. "Skip-

per,'' he said, ''I think the Animal killed one of
them.''

''Now, just how in the hell did that happen?'' asked
Tynan, exasperated.

''They ran up on us and one of them fired at us.
Hit Ross in the side, but it was more of a scratch than
anything else. Barely broke the skin. Animal emptied
a magazine at them to turn them around. He was trying
to scare them away.''

There was a rippling of fire behind them and then
from in front of them. Tynan could hear the rounds
slamming into the trunks of the palms near him.
Slowly the shooting tapered off until the jungle was
quiet again except for the screaming of the animals
scared by all the shooting.

''Sterne,'' said Tynan, ''we're going to pull out to
the south. Half a klick, maybe a little more. You take
off and see what's in front of us.''

Sterne nodded and began to crawl away. When he
had vanished in the vegetation, Tynan said, ''Let's
get back to the rest of the team.''

They found the others crouching among the trees
and bushes, their eyes on the jungle. Ross lay on his
back, his pack and equipment beside him, his shirt
pulled up to reveal his nearly invisible wound. The
angry red welt had bled little. Ross dabbed at it with
a piece of gauze ripped from a larger bandage from
one of the first-aid kits.

Tynan crept to him and asked, ''Can you move?''

''Christ, Skipper, this is nothing,'' he said. ''Burns
more than anything.''

''Okay. Get saddled up.'' Tynan crawled off and
warned the rest of the team that they were going to
withdraw to the south. Jones would lead them until
they caught up with Sterne; Tynan would take the
rear.

"I'll stick with you, Skipper," said Boone.

Tynan was about to protest and then thought better of it. "Good," he said.

As the others withdrew, Ross carrying his share of the equipment, Tynan leaned close to Boone. He said, "When our men are clear, I want to put a volley into both camps, firing high so that we don't hit anyone. I want to give them something to think about."

Then, coming from the direction of the militia, Tynan heard voices. There was a rustling of branches as the men worked their way forward. Finally a voice shouted, in French, "Who are you?"

Instead of answering, Tynan said, "Now."

Both opened fired with their AK-47s, hosing down the trees around them, spraying rounds over everyone's head, trying to force the militia to retreat. When the weapons were empty, Tynan waved at Boone, telling him to get out. Cautiously they both retreated, moving south, toward the rest of the team.

Just as they fled, firing erupted again as the two groups of militia shot it out with each other. There was a single, sharp explosion, as if one of them had had a grenade and had used it. The sound of the firing increased in volume until it was a steady hammering.

Tynan grinned at Boone. "I guess we stirred them up some."

They hurried on until they caught up with the rest of the team. Sterne had halted them in a thick stand of palm that commanded the surrounding area. When Tynan and Boone arrived a few minutes later, the sounds of the battle still echoed behind them.

As they entered the tiny perimeter Sterne asked, "What the hell did you do, Skipper?"

Tynan ignored the question. He said, "We can assume one of two things. Either we fooled them and they'll soon realize they're shooting up their own men and quit, never realizing there was a third party in the area, or we didn't fool them.''

"Which means?" asked Boone.

"Which means we need to get out of here. And, since we've got one wounded, it probably means they saw us. They're going to know that we pulled a fast one. They're going to bring in help to look for us.''

"So we had better get the fuck out of here," said Sterne.

"I would think," said Tynan, "that it would be a good idea.''

Tynan glanced at his watch and then upward, toward the sun. It was now very late in the morning, but they couldn't take time to eat. The men would just have to wait for a couple of hours more.

"Sterne," he said, "south again for another half klick, and then back to the east." He crouched, pulled out his map, and examined it closely. "We're now south and west of where we want to be. We'll have to adjust for that later.''

"Aye, aye, Skipper," said Sterne.

Again Sterne took off, entering the thickest part of the jungle, now being careful not to leave any signs. Instead of hacking at the clinging vines, he yanked his feet free of them. He pushed branches aside, raking his hands on their thorns, sometimes dropping to his hands and knees to get under obstacles. The pace was slower than it had been, but it was more tiring, since he had to fight the jungle nearly every step of the way. Sterne was soon breathing hard, as if he had just run a half a klick rather than walked it.

He came to a stream and stopped. The vegetation dipped into the water, which was crystal clear. A large stone stuck through the surface in about the middle of the stream. Sterne was sure that he could leap to it and then to the other bank without leaving any sign.

Of course, the water was moving fast enough that any silt he stirred up would quickly dissipate. His footprints in the soft bottom would fill in and vanish in minutes.

Just as he was about to break cover, he heard the distant popping of rotor blades. In Vietnam it would have meant that Americans were near. Here, in Africa, it could only be bad news. He retreated deeper into the cover of the jungle, his eyes locked on the tiny patch of sky that he could see through the dense foliage.

He heard a noise behind him and turned in time to see Tynan there. He waved a hand, motioning Tynan to stay. Then he circled a hand over his head and pointed toward the sky. The noise of the helicopter was louder now. It was coming closer.

He saw Tynan nod his understanding and then hold up a hand, telling the rest of the team to stay put.

Sterne turned his attention back to the sky. The sound of the chopper's engines had faded for a moment, and then it came back, as if it were searching for something. Overhead, he saw a flash of light as the sun glinted off the windshield. He put a hand to his eyes to shade them and saw the helicopter briefly. He didn't recognize it because it wasn't an American Huey or Chinook. It was of French design, he thought, but he just didn't know.

Finally Tynan crept forward and crouched next to him. Silently they watched the sky, the chopper flashing past periodically. Then its engines faded.

"Let's get across the stream," said Tynan impatiently. He didn't like the cat-and-mouse game anymore. It was too difficult to play. Dodging everything and everyone. For the first time he had an appreciation for the Viet Cong. They had similar problems, although they did have allies in South Vietnam. They could count on support from some villages and they did blend in with the local population, so that you couldn't be sure who was the enemy and who wasn't. Here, Tynan's men all stood out, they had no allies at all, and everyone was an enemy. The only help he could count on was a ship that was now fifty or sixty miles off the coast.

He looked at his map again and realized that he had only made ten, twelve klicks from the coast. Maybe six or seven miles, and at this rate it could be three days before they reached the crash site, provided the information they had was correct. He just didn't have time to fool around. That chopper suggested that the local government was looking for the plane, and if that was true, it could also be true that the Soviets were searching.

Before Sterne could protest the order, Tynan said, "I'll move the others up to this point. You find somewhere on the other side where we can regroup. You better grab a bite too, because we're not going to stop for lunch. Eat when you can."

Sterne nodded but didn't speak. Tynan watched him crawl forward toward the bank of the stream, test the ground for his footing, and then hop to the large rock in the center. He waved his arms wildly for a moment, as if he were going to fall in, then regained his balance. He leaped to the other bank and quickly disappeared into the jungle. A second later, Tynan saw Sterne's smiling face as he waved him forward.

Quietly Tynan returned to the main body of the patrol and urged them forward. He got them to the bank of the stream and told them to jump to the rock and then to the other side. Jones, carrying the heavy radio, some of the explosive, and his personal weapon, leaped first. He landed solidly on the rock and then jumped to the opposite bank. Sterne's arm shot out of the vegetation and dragged him to cover.

As Ross moved to the bank the helicopter reappeared. Ross dived back into the undergrowth and lay still, almost as if he had been killed. The chopper circled them once, and through a gap in the trees Tynan could see the face of one of the pilots. He was surprised because there was a white man in the cockpit of the aircraft. It could only be bad news, because it seemed to underscore the idea that the Soviets were working with the locals. Tynan knew it meant he would have to be that much more careful.

But apparently the men in the chopper had seen nothing, because the craft turned and vanished in the north. Tynan signaled Ross out of cover. He jumped for the rock, slipped, and plunged into the water. He put out a hand, trying to break his fall. He stumbled forward a step and then fell to his knees, soaking himself. He scrambled back to his feet and up the bank into the jungle.

Tynan looked at the large stain of stirred-up mud and silt as it began to dissipate, swirling downstream. To the others he said, "Let's go." He jumped into the water, ignoring the rock that Sterne had used, and hurried across. At no point was the stream very deep.

On that side of the stream, they didn't rest. Sterne pointed to a narrow game trail he had found. There was no evidence that any of the large predators of Africa used it. Tynan thought that the lions hunted mainly on the savannas and it was only in the Tarzan movies they roamed the jungle preying on people. He knew that there were no tigers in Africa, something else the Tarzan movies didn't know.

They hadn't traveled very far when Tynan heard Sterne's voice.

"Shit!" he said. It was followed by three quick shots and Sterne saying "Shit!" again.

The men dived from the trail, rolling under the bushes and behind the trees along it, their weapons ready. Tynan crawled along the side of it, watching and listening. In seconds he could see Sterne, his weapon pointed downward.

Tynan got to his feet and moved closer. "Now what the hell?" he asked.

"Fucking snake," said Sterne. "I didn't see it hanging on the branch until I was nearly on top of it. Couldn't do anything but shoot."

Tynan looked at the snake. It was ten or twelve feet long, with a thick head that had been shredded by one of the AK rounds. About four feet behind the head, the snake had been blown nearly in half by Sterne's first two shots. It still twitched, but it was obvious that it was dead.

Tynan took off his cap and ran a hand through his sweat-damp hair. "I don't know about this," he said. "We keep fucking it up. You shouldn't have shot that damned thing."

"I know that," snapped Sterne. "It surprised me. I didn't think."

"Just shut up and let *me* think," said Tynan. He was quiet for a moment while his mind raced. No one knew for sure that they were there. That Americans were searching for the plane. Three shots in the jungle couldn't be all that unusual. It might not be as disastrous as it seemed at first. Not with everything else going on.

"Take the point again, and pick up the pace. We've got to get a couple of klicks away from here. Then we'll stop for a while and watch our trail."

"Aye, aye, Skipper." Sterne turned to go but stopped. "Sorry about the snake. I shouldn't have shot it, but it just sort of popped up in front of me."

"Don't worry about it. Just get going."

Tynan returned to the rest of the patrol, told them about the snake and how Sterne had shot it, and got them moving. They hiked deeper into the jungle, following the game trail, but now more alert for the natural dangers that might lurk along it. They walked rapidly, each step becoming a burden as they hurried toward the Blackbird. Their feet became leaden, and it was soon a test of endurance. Who would be the first to collapse under the strain? Who would be the first to fall? They were all breathing hard, heavily; their mouths seemed to be jammed with cotton. Sweat poured from them, rolling down their faces and into the collars of their already soaked shirts. They fought the heat and humidity, soon forgetting everything except the heat.

Overhead, the sun climbed to its peak and began to drop away. Clouds appeared, vanished, and re-formed. By late afternoon, the sky was overcast with gray clouds drifting over the angry black ones. Rain threatened, and they heard the far-off rumble of thunder, not unlike the sound of a distant B-52 strike in Vietnam.

As the rain hit them, at first a few cooling drops and then sudden sheets of water, Tynan called a halt. It was hard enough to move quietly through the jungle avoiding all the local people, but the sound of the rain covered too much noise. They might walk right into an enemy camp, and that was the last thing they needed.

They scattered, searching for some shelter under the broad leaves of the palms, but the rain was too heavy and coming down too fast. All they could do was sit in the mud and watch as everything around them was soaked. And wait. Wait for it to end so that they could move out again.

9

It was just after noon when Molodin received the bad news. He was eating field rations, the men of his search party scattered around him under the shade of the trees. He looked up when the major approached him.

"My men," he began, "have reported a group of whites near the coast."

Molodin swallowed his food, jammed the metal spoon into the ration can, and asked, "Why do you tell me this?"

"They have fired on my men. Then they ran away, and we do not know where they have gone."

"Show me on the map," said Molodin as he got to his feet. He headed toward a truck parked under one of the large palm trees that bordered the rough road.

Studying the map carefully, the major finally pointed to a place not far from the coast. "Here," he said. "They were near here."

"Yes," said Molodin. He thought quickly. Since the major was concerned, it meant that the white men were of unknown origin. Granted that the customs office and borders weren't all that well guarded, but the coincidence of a group of unknown whites entering at that moment was too much to ignore.

"What have you done about this?" Molodin asked the major.

"Our president has granted us the use of one helicopter and we have flown over the area. There has been no report from it. The pilot has seen nothing."

"I believe," said Molodin, "that our search is too far to the east and too far to the north. The Americans would not try to walk a hundred miles to the crash site. We must shift our search to the west and south."

The major straightened. "I will see to it."

"Let's put our men back on the trucks and move them. Then I believe you should return to the airport and collect the other members of our party. We shall be at the crash site soon now. The Americans have told us where to look."

When the rain ended, Tynan didn't feel like moving. He just wanted to sit in the mud and wait for something to happen. Although they had left the ship less than twenty-four hours earlier, he was already tired, nearly exhausted. It would have been easy to sit there, although it wouldn't have been very comfortable.

But, just as he had known as he scrambled under the fence in Scotland, he couldn't sit there. Sterne had been on point all morning. In Vietnam it was a good idea to rotate the point to keep the men alert, but here Tynan wasn't sure that it was necessary. He sent Sterne out again, telling him to head nearly due east and divert only to avoid obstacles that would delay them.

With the trees still dripping rain and the ground steaming, the light, white mist obscuring little, they moved east. Tynan kept Sterne in sight now, afraid that all the delays and all the shooting would have alerted the locals. Maybe even caused the locals to send out search parties to look for Tynan and his men. Strung out behind him was the rest of his patrol. They were walking slowly, stumbling forward, their heads bowed, as if they had been marching for weeks instead of hours. The heat and humidity did that to men who were unaccustomed to the tropics. Even Tynan, with his recent tour in Vietnam, was beginning to feel it.

For an hour they moved through the jungle. It was late in the day when Sterne dropped to the ground and began crawling forward. Tynan rushed after him, crouched, and then saw, through the trees, what had interested Sterne.

Twenty or thirty men, dressed like those they had seen earlier in the day, were camped in a clearing. To his left, he could see Sterne watching the men. Then Sterne began to creep backward, away from the clearing.

Suddenly there was a whoop from the clearing and the men began scrambling about, grabbing their rifles. They swarmed toward where Tynan and Sterne hid; then they halted and rushed the other way for a moment.

Sterne froze at the first sound. When the men turned, he crawled quickly to Tynan, but before he could say a word, the men in the clearing rallied and rushed them.

For an instant Tynan considered fleeing, but then firing erupted in front of him. Tynan grabbed his own weapon, flipped off the safety, and squeezed off a short burst.

The attacking men dived for cover, shouting and screaming, some of it in French, some in English, and much of it in their native tongue. They began shooting into the jungle, firing at anything that moved. Tynan saw a monkey drop from a tree near him, crashing down through the small branches until it smacked the ground.

Sterne got close enough to ask, "What now?"

"I think we're trapped this time. Get Boone and Jones up here, and have Animal and Ross cover the rear."

"We going to stand and fight?"

"We're going to try to push them back," said Tynan. "A little disciplined fire ought to scare them out of here."

"We shoot to kill instead of over their heads?"

"If they rush us, we do what we have to. We don't let them overrun us."

"Aye, aye, sir!"

As Sterne went to give the others their instructions Tynan reached forward and unfastened the bayonet that was stowed under the barrel of his weapon. He locked it into place and then waited.

Sterne returned with the other two men, and Tynan spread them through the trees with orders not to shoot unless the enemy rushed them. The firing had tapered to the periodic pop of a single weapon, as if the enemy were trying to find Tynan and his men by making them shoot back.

There was a moment of silence, and then the militiamen swarmed from their hiding positions, yelling and shooting.

"Pick your targets," Tynan commanded. "Single shot. Pick your targets."

This was the last thing that Tynan wanted. He had tried to avoid a fight, but now he had no choice. He didn't want to shoot at the men rushing at him. They had done nothing but be in the wrong place at the wrong time. Somehow they had spotted Sterne and decided that they wanted a fight. Now Tynan couldn't avoid it.

To his right he heard Sterne fire once, twice, and then begin to shoot rapidly. To the left Boone and Jones opened fire together, cutting down two of the black men before they had taken more than a couple of steps.

Tynan got to one knee, using the trunk of a palm for cover, and sighted on a large man who was leaping over a fallen tree. Tynan hesitated and then pulled the trigger. He saw the bullet hit the man, spin him, knocking him to the ground. He started to get up, grabbed at his chest, and fell back, screaming.

Another man appeared near the fallen tree. Tynan fired at him and missed. The man dived for cover and began sniping at Tynan, his rounds peeling the bark from the palm tree where Tynan hid.

To the right, Tynan saw a man trying to climb into the low branches of one of the trees. He aimed carefully and dropped him with a single shot.

Shouting came from the enemy lines and the shooting tapered off. Men who had been pressing close to Tynan's group fell back through the clearing to the jungle on the other side. They seemed on the verge of a full retreat, running rapidly, but instead of fleeing the area, they dived for cover and began firing at Tynan's men.

The shooting wasn't accurate. The bullets were whining overhead, slicing through the leaves of the palms, chipping away at the trunks of the trees, but not coming close to Tynan and his men.

Sterne continued to return fire, his shots well spaced. He was rewarded with a piercing scream.

"Hold your fire," said Tynan. "Hold your fire."

He sat back for a moment, considering everything. There was no way that he could afford to be pinned down. If he were still in Vietnam, the solution would be to call in artillery, but that option was out. Even

if he could get the ship back into range, there was just
no way that a United States naval vessel could shell
a foreign nation.

The only way to end the fight was to attack. The
enemy had shown that they didn't understand military
tactics. A frontal assault across the open ground was
ridiculous. Tynan turned and said to his men, "Flank
them. Flank them."

No one responded. Tynan saw Sterne begin to crawl
off to the right. He turned in time to see Jones disappear into the jungle in that direction.

Tynan began firing into the jungle in front of him,
drawing a heavy return. He ducked, let it fall off, and
then threw a few more rounds at the militia.

Within minutes, Tynan heard the AKs open fire
again. He crawled forward to the edge of the clearing
and switched to full auto, raking the trees. For a
moment there was an increase in the firing, but it
quickly ended. There was screaming from among the
trees, and then a crashing as the survivors fled through
the jungle.

As the firing ended, Tynan stepped over the fallen
tree. He saw the man he had shot lying on his side,
both hands pressed to his stomach as he tried to hold
his intestines in. He looked up, his face twisted in
pain, the whites of his eyes yellowed. Blood trickled
from his mouth, and his breathing was rapid and shallow. Tynan knew that the man didn't have long to
live. He crouched by him, tossed the man's rifle into
the trees, out of his reach, and then attempted to
examine the wound.

The man tried to pull away, gasped once, and fell
back, his eyes pleading.

"Let me see," said Tynan quietly, but the man
didn't understand.

Jones appeared across the clearing. He stared at Tynan for a moment and then called, "What do we do with the wounded?"

Tynan looked at the bleeding man near him. There was absolutely nothing he could do to help, and the kindest thing would be to put a bullet through the man's head. But Tynan knew he couldn't do that because no one outside the military would understand the gesture. It was bad enough that he had shot up the local militia, but then to shoot the wounded would cause repercussions in the UN and the Congress.

Tynan glanced at the man a final time, making sure that he had no weapon near him, and then left him. He crossed the clearing quickly. Jones led him into the trees. They came to a man sitting with his back against a palm. He had a belt wrapped around his thigh, drawn tight. There was a ragged crimson stain on his khaki pants.

Near them was another man, lying on his side, clutching his arm. A bullet had smashed the bone, some of which was visible through the wound.

Sterne was standing over a third man, who had a large bandage wrapped around his head. His eyes were slightly unfocused, as if he were just regaining consciousness.

There was a fourth man, lying on his back, his chest heaving as he fought for breath. He had been shot three or four times; his shirt was soaked with blood. As Tynan watched, the man spasmed and died.

To Jones, he said, "Do what you can for them. Leave some food and water, and then let's get the hell out of here."

"You sure?"

"Yes. We can't take them with us, and we sure as hell can't shoot them. Their friends know where they are. Maybe they'll return in a little while."

"That would suggest that we definitely need to get out of here," said Sterne.

"This is not a combat environment," said Tynan. "We do what we can as fast as we can, and then we split."

As Jones tried to help the wounded, Tynan went back to get Ross and Hollinger. Then they checked the men who had assaulted across the open ground. They found six bodies and one other wounded who had tried to crawl into hiding. He struggled when Tynan and Ross tried to get in to help him. Finally they gave up, tossing a field dressing at him.

They hurried back across the clearing, joined up with Jones, Sterne, and Boone. Tynan looked at them and then said, "Boone, you want to take the point for a while?"

"Sure, Skipper."

"Still due east. I think we've about twenty miles to go before we reach the crash site."

"Won't make it before dark," said Jones. "It's way too late now."

"If nothing else," said Tynan, "we've got to get clear of here. Well clear. If we push on through most of the night, we can be close enough to find the plane tomorrow."

Boone started off, but Tynan stopped him. He looked at Sterne and Jones and asked, "Is there anything else you can do for the wounded?"

"We've done all we can," said Jones.

"Okay, Boone. Take off."

They strung out again, filtering through the trees, now avoiding the trails that they came to because they knew that others were in the vicinity who would soon be looking for them.

About sundown, Tynan called a halt. They had been on the move all day and hadn't even taken time to eat. Now they had to rest. The strain was beginning to show. Tynan made sure that they had a perimeter established, with everyone watching everyone else, and then sat down to eat. The food didn't appeal to him. Cold canned food rarely did. He sprinkled it liberally with salt and ate it slowly. He drank part of his water ration, realizing that he would run out of water by noon the next day. More problems to worry about.

After thirty minutes, he got the men on their feet and moving again. Night fell with a crash rather than the gradual loss of light experienced in the Northern Hemisphere. It seemed that one minute there was enough light to see by and the next it was nearly pitch black. Boone stopped long enough to cut a walking stick and then moved out again.

The pace faltered because of the night. The men stumbled on, moving carefully to avoid the trees. The moon came up, providing some light for them, showing them the jungle in a variety of grays, blacks, and deeper blacks.

About midnight, Boone stopped. Tynan caught up to him and leaned near him. "What's the problem?"

"No problem, Skipper," he said. "I think we're here."

"What?"

Boone stepped forward and pulled back the branch of a large bush. Tynan could see a huge shape lying at an angle, a couple of trees crushed under it. Even with the cold half-light of the moon, it was hard to tell what they were looking at. Tynan knew instinctively that Boone was right. They had arrived.

"I guess the boys in Washington got the distances wrong. We shouldn't be near it yet."

"No, sir, but that certainly is the Blackbird."

10

It seemed to Tynan that he had only been asleep for a matter of minutes. He wasn't rested and his eyes still felt like someone had thrown a handful of sand into them. He had spent an hour organizing the position, finally finding a good hiding place under one of the crumpled wings, and then spreading the men out, into the jungle around them. Ross and Hollinger had been eager to start placing the explosives, but Tynan had feared a mistake in the dark and he didn't want to show a light. Given the situation, he felt they could wait until morning and by noon the job should have been done.

Now he sat in the early-morning dark, trying to see anything that might be concealed by the night, and listening to Jones, who crouched next to him. Jones had whispered something that Tynan just hadn't heard.

"I said that I thought I heard someone moving in the jungle near us," Jones said.

"You sure?"

"No, sir. I said I think I did."

"In what direction?"

Jones pointed to the northeast and said, "Over there. Quiet sounds, like someone trying to sneak through the jungle. I didn't figure it for an animal. It was too quiet. Making too little noise."

Tynan wasn't sure that Jones was right about the noise being too quiet for an animal, but he respected his instincts. He said, "You wake the others. I'll see what I can find out."

As Jones began to circulate to wake the others Tynan, leaving his equipment behind except for his weapon and a couple of spare magazines, edged his way around the remains of the plane, toward where Jones had heard the noise. Tynan moved slowly, placing each foot carefully, cautiously putting his weight on it so that he didn't make a sound. It took him ten minutes to move fifty meters. He was under the wing of the plane when he heard something and froze.

He turned his head to the left, cocking his ear and staring out of the corners of his eyes. Training had taught him that night vision worked better that way and his experience in the field had confirmed it.

The quiet rustling came again, and Tynan had to agree that it didn't sound like an animal. Tynan slowly crouched until he was resting on one knee, his weapon held in both hands. He thought he saw a flash of movement, but in the dark, with shifting shadows caused by a light breeze, he couldn't be sure of it.

Then, almost as if to confirm that someone was out there, he heard a hushed curse in a language that he couldn't identify. The voice had spoken so quietly that Tynan had been sure only that it was someone speaking.

A shape loomed at his side, and Tynan turned toward it. He put a restraining hand on Sterne's shoulder and put his lips close to his ear. "Jones was right. There is someone out there."

"What'll we do about them, Skipper?"

Tynan nodded to the rear and stood up. He began to walk away, toward the tail of the plane where the others would be assembled.

When he got there, he saw that all the men were waiting for him. He asked, "How long to rig the plane?"

"Depends on exactly what you want as an end result," said Hollinger.

"I want little tiny pieces that will be of no use to anyone for anything. Little bitty pieces that will be hard to see without a microscope. I want total destruction, and if you could get it to burn, too, that would be perfect."

Hollinger hesitated before he answered. He looked at Ross, who shrugged. Finally Hollinger said, "In the daylight and if the internal systems can be repaired easily, maybe an hour and a half, maybe two."

"Both of you or only one?" asked Tynan.

"I should be able to handle it alone," said Hollinger quietly.

"Here's what I want to do," said Tynan. "Hollinger should stay here, hidden, and as soon as the sun comes up prepare to blow up the plane."

"The equipment in it, Skipper," interrupted Jones.

"Fuck the equipment. Nobody said shit about recovering equipment. We blow the whole thing up. While he's doing that the rest of us will try to draw the search party off, back to the north and east if possible. When we hear the explosion, we'll try to lose the enemy and divert back to the west, heading for the beach where we came ashore to prepare for the scheduled exfiltration."

"And what do I do, Skipper?" asked Hollinger.

"As soon as the plane goes up, you head straight to the beach and wait for us there."

"How are you going to lead them off?"

"Get behind them and make a little noise so that they'll spot us, and then we'll just run away from them. If they're searching for the plane, they may assume that we know where it is and try following us until we get to it. By the time they realize we're just running around the jungle having a good time on our hike, it should be too late. Any questions?''

''I don't have much spare ammo for my weapon, Skipper,'' said Hollinger.

''You shouldn't need much. All you have to do is blow up the plane. You're not going to shoot anyone.''

''And what if you don't make it to the beach, or I don't make it in time?''

''We'll wait for you,'' said Tynan, ''but if for some reason we don't meet, work your way to the capital and report to the American Embassy there. Tell the chargé d'affaires who you are and tell him to confirm with Wheeler in London.''

''Aye, aye, sir.''

Tynan said, ''Everyone grab your gear. Leave all the explosives here for Hollinger. We move out in five minutes. And we have to remain quiet,'' he cautioned them. ''If they suspect what we're doing, the whole plan unravels.''

Less than five minutes later they were ready. Sterne took the point again and Boone brought up the rear. They maintained a very short interval, each man being able to see the man in front of him and the shape of the next one in the line. They headed out straight north, moving rapidly in the dark. Finally they turned to the east and then veered south, trying to find the rear of the other formation.

They hadn't gone far when Sterne stopped. Tynan eased forward and whispered, ''What's the problem?''

''No problem, Skipper. They've stopped. Camped. I think they're going to eat breakfast. What'll we do?''

"Let them get settled in good and then we'll pull out, back to the north, making noise so that they'll hear us and try to follow. We'll interrupt their breakfast. That ought to really piss them off."

From the jungle in front of them Tynan could hear a quiet rattling of equipment as the men of the other patrol settled in. There was talking in hushed tones, the sounds drifting toward Tynan, but again he couldn't make out the words. He thought that it sounded like Russian, but he was afraid that he was letting his mind play tricks on him.

Tynan checked his watch and discovered that sunrise was thirty minutes away. He crawled to Boone and said, "You wait here and see what happens. Don't let them see you, but if they don't take the bait, you'll have to let me know."

"Aye, aye, sir."

He worked his way back to Sterne and said, "Head due north. Give me three minutes before you head out."

Sterne nodded his understanding.

Tynan then alerted the rest of his team. Finally he stood up and said in a normal tone of voice, "Let's move it. We've got a mission to complete."

Sterne turned to stare at him, surprised at the sudden sound of Tynan's voice. Tynan waved at him, signaling him to move out. The rest of them, minus Boone, started forward. Sterne didn't try to keep quiet; he just crashed through the jungle, pushing aside the leafy branches of bushes and hacking at some of the vines with his machete.

A few minutes later, Boone caught up with them. As they continued to march north he told Tynan, "You should have seen them when you opened your mouth. It was like someone tossed a grenade at them. People scrambling all over."

"How many were there?"

"Couldn't get a good count, but I did see three white guys with them. Maybe fifteen or twenty blacks."

"And they're following?" asked Tynan.

"As far as I know. I took off when a couple of them started toward where I was hiding. We going to ambush them?"

"No, of course not. All we have to do is lead them away from the plane until the Animal can get the charges rigged. Then it doesn't matter."

Tynan skipped ahead, catching up with Sterne. "We've got to make a little better time," he said. "I don't want the opposition getting too close to us."

"Aye, aye," said Sterne. He picked up the pace as the sun finally appeared and the ground began to brighten. He could see obstacles in the way and avoided them. He used his machete more, hacking at vines and bushes, trying to leave a trail that anyone could follow. Occasionally he glanced at the sky, a deep blue, visible through gaps in the jungle. He tried to keep the sun to his right, heading north.

He came to a small stream and leaped it. He crouched on the opposite bank for an instant. There was a sudden screeching around him as the monkeys woke for the new day. That noise was joined by birds screaming their displeasure. In the riot of sound, Sterne could hear nothing other than the animals and birds. He got to his feet, scrambled up the slight rise near the stream, and disappeared into the vegetation.

Tynan ranged up and down the line of his patrol, making sure that everyone was still with them. He watched Ross stagger forward, looking as if he were about to collapse, but he told Tynan that he always looked that bad. Boone had dropped off and waited until he saw movement behind them. He had then scampered forward and told Tynan that they were still being followed.

For the next hour they hurried through the jungle. The sun came up, burning away the last chill of the night, soon baking them. Tynan found himself covered with sweat quickly. His skin began to itch because he hadn't had the opportunity to wash away the sweat from the day before. He ignored the minor irritation and followed Sterne, breathing through his mouth because the pace was so fast.

The rapid pace came to a screaming halt minutes later. Tynan saw Sterne standing near a wall of vegetation. He ran up to him and said, "Now what?"

"I'm afraid we're boxed in."

"Push on through. We don't have to maintain a big lead, we just have to stay in front."

"Can't push through, Skipper," said Sterne. "It's a stone wall, fifty, sixty meters high."

Tynan looked at his watch. He could hear the men around him, breathing deeply, each still standing, waiting to take off again, but each thankful for the few moments of rest. He turned and studied them. Time was no longer a problem. They had been heading away from the crash for over an hour. Hollinger should have the plane rigged, and any moment Tynan would hear the explosions telling him the mission was over. They had done their job by leading the enemy unit away.

"All right, let's take a break. Boone, keep your eye on our trail. Everyone grab a bite to eat."

They fanned out in a semicircle anchored against the rock cliff. Boone was in front of them, sitting behind a large palm tree, watching the trail. He could hear people moving, but he could see nothing of them. If they had been in Vietnam, Boone would have been worried about that, but they were in Africa. He sat

there, trying to look calm as he ate his breakfast of
cold scrambled eggs from a C-ration can.

After Tynan finished his breakfast, he moved around
the perimeter, checking on the men. Each of them
was tired, but they were used to having to operate
under the strain of combat conditions. Here it was a
little less stressful because it wasn't combat. The thing
that bothered him the most was that he still hadn't
heard the explosions from the crash site.

He stopped near Ross to ask, "Shouldn't the Animal have blown up the Blackbird by now?"

Ross was sitting on a rotting log, using a white
plastic spoon to eat peaches from a C-ration can. He
chewed slowly, as if considering the question, glanced
at his watch, and said, "I would think that it will go
up any second now. You wanted him to wait until we
were clear of the area and it was light enough to see."

"How soon?"

"I don't know, Skipper. Given the circumstances,
I would think it'll go up any minute."

"Will we be able to hear it?"

Ross sighed and dropped his spoon into the syrup
from the peaches. He set the can on the log beside
him. "I would think that we'll be able to hear it.
Anyone within fifteen, twenty miles should hear it.
We haven't come that far, have we?"

Tynan rubbed his eyes. He took out his map. It was
now tattered from wear, and damp from yesterday's
rain and Tynan's sweat. He studied it but could find
nothing to suggest they should have run into a cliff.
Still, given everything, he was sure that they were no
more than seven or eight miles from the crash site. If
that far.

"No," he told Ross, "we haven't come that far."

"When it goes," said Ross, "we'll hear it."

Tynan left Ross then, moving back to where Jones sat quietly, his eyes closed. Tynan was going to ask him how the radio was but decided to let Jones sleep. He held a half-eaten Hershey bar in his hand, and Tynan wondered how he managed to keep it from turning to liquid in the heat of the jungle.

Tynan took a drink from his nearly empty canteen. He watched Boone creep toward him, dodging from bush to bush, as if trying to stay under cover.

"Skipper," he said when he was close, "they've stopped. I think they're trying to outflank us."

"Who is?"

"The guys following us. I can hear them out there, but they haven't come into view. It's like they're setting up a perimeter and then will attack us."

"Then they're playing into our hands," said Tynan. "Every second they waste screwing around in the jungle means that much longer for them to get back to the plane and that much more time the Animal has."

"But if they're setting up for an attack . . ."

"Don't worry about it," said Tynan. "They are not going to come in here, guns blazing."

"So what do we do?"

"We sit quietly and let them make a move. Time is our ally, not theirs."

Neither spoke for the next few minutes. The only sounds were the animals in the trees and the birds overhead. There was a light breeze that did little.

Tynan studied his watch, the second hand creeping around while the minutes dragged. He was waiting for the rumble of the distant explosion telling him that the plane was gone, but it didn't come. He reviewed what Ross had said about needing the time to rig it right, but both had estimated two hours at the most. Hollinger should have had time to do the job by now.

Then, from the jungle, a voice called, "American soldiers. American soldiers. I know that you are there."

Tynan dived to the right, grabbing his weapon and pointing it at the sound. He saw that the other men had vanished from sight, each taking any available cover. Ross was hugging the ground near him, watching him. Tynan shrugged to tell him that he didn't know what the hell was happening.

"American soldiers. We know that you are there. You should talk to us."

Tynan wasn't sure what to do. He had been ready for a number of things, but this wasn't one of them. He rubbed a hand over his face, looked at the sweat on it, and then wiped it on his fatigue jacket.

Ross raised an eyebrow in question.

Tynan shrugged in response.

"American soldiers, you should know that we have your demolitions man. He failed in his mission."

Tynan felt his stomach flip over. "That fucking tears it," he muttered.

"What are you going to do now, American soldiers?" asked the voice.

A fucking good question, Tynan said to himself.

11

For several seconds no one breathed. No one moved.
Tynan stared into the jungle in front of him but could
see nothing other than the trees and bushes and vines.
A brightly colored bird sat near the top of one, unmov-
ing, as if watching everything that was going on below
it.

Finally the voice came again. "American soldiers.
There is nothing that you can do. Why not come out?
We will escort you to the coast and see that you are
not harmed."

Ross looked up from where he was hidden and asked
quietly, "We going to take the deal?"

"Fuck, no," said Tynan. "Not until that plane is
a memory. Now let me think."

If he knew exactly where the enemy soldiers were,
he might be able to sneak through their lines. If he
waited until dark, he figured he could elude them easily and get back to the plane, but now time was on
the enemy's side, not his. The longer he was pinned
against the cliff, the more time they had to get someone into the field to learn the secrets of the Blackbird.
Now he had to hurry.

"A diversion," he whispered. "We need a diver-

sion so that you can get out of here and try to reach
the plane and blow the fucker up.''

Ross nodded.

"You and Sterne. Get out of here." Tynan turned
so that he could study the cliff face behind them. He
couldn't really see the rock because of the vegetation
that grew from the cracks and hung down from the
top. It would be a hell of a climb, especially for some-
onc trying not to be seen, but it could be done. The
vegetation growing on it was thick enough and the
enemy was far enough away that the jungle would
provide more screening. Once on top, they could split
in whatever direction they wanted.

"American soldiers. You are beginning to try my
patience severely.''

"Sterne," called Tynan quietly. "Sterne, get your
ass over here.''

In a moment Sterne slipped to the ground near
Tynan. "What do you need, Skipper?''

"I want you to take Ross to the plane and blow it
up. I don't care what you have to do to get him there,
but I want that aircraft destroyed.''

"If I run into militia?''

"Do I have to spell it out for you?" snapped Tynan.
"The plane is to be destroyed. All other considera-
tions are secondary. Let Washington sort out the bodies afterwards. That clear enough?''

"Aye, aye, Skipper.''

"Delay does you no good, American soldiers," said
the voice. "We will come to get you.''

Tynan looked at the jungle, where the voice came
from, but still could see no people. He turned his
attention back to Sterne. "You'll have to work your
way up the face of the cliff, trying to keep out of
sight.''

"That won't be easy.''

"I didn't say that it was going to be easy. We'll try to create a diversion down here. When it begins, you move out."

"Aye, aye."

"American soldiers, we know that you are there. Why don't you talk to me?"

"You have three minutes to get ready," said Tynan. "Then I start the diversion."

Without a word, Sterne turned and began to crawl backward, toward the rock cliff. Tynan watched him as he explored the surface hidden by the deep green vegetation. Ross, dragging a satchel of explosives, followed behind him. After a moment, both of them disappeared from sight.

Tynan worked his way from the log to where Boone crouched. Boone shot him a glance and said, "I thought I heard someone moving in that direction. Over there, in the trees. But I didn't see them."

"Over there?" asked Tynan, pointing with the barrel of his AK-47.

"Somewhere over there," agreed Boone. "Couldn't really tell."

"Fine." Tynan got to his knees and took the safety off his weapon. He aimed about twenty feet up the trunk of a tree and pulled the trigger. The short burst slammed into the palm, stripping bark from it.

The panicked shout came from far to the right. "Hey, American soldiers! Don't shoot at us! We mean you no harm. Stop the shooting and let's talk."

"Pull your people back, out of here," shouted Tynan in response.

"Sure. We can do that. But why don't you come out and talk to us, American soldiers? It is so much easier than shouting through the jungle."

"We are not American soldiers," responded Tynan. Well, it wasn't a complete lie. They might be Americans, but technically they weren't soldiers but sailors.

"It does not matter who you are."

"What do you want?" asked Tynan.

"You know what we want. You must come out and surrender to us. We will take you to the coast so that you can leave this country. You are here illegally."

Tynan turned to look at the rock cliff, but Sterne and Ross were lost in the vines and bushes growing from it. He heard nothing from them but assumed that they had begun the climb when the shooting started. How long would it take? Did the people shouting at him know how many men Tynan had? Were there enemy soldiers on top of the cliff?

As soon as he heard the burst from the AK-47, Sterne started the climb. He had found a large crack in the rock face that sprouted a couple of bushes. Sterne slung his rifle and reached out, grabbing a bush near the base where the trunk was thick. He put his foot on the crack and hauled himself up, forcing himself between the branches and the rock. He slid beyond it, eased himself upward, and seized the next. Behind that bush the crack narrowed and then disappeared, but above him was another. He grasped the thick, rough stone, chinning himself. With his foot he searched for toeholds, using the strength of his legs to push himself upward, staying behind the concealing foliage of the bushes.

When he got to the new level, he stopped. Just below him, slightly to the side, was Ross, who was having a little trouble climbing upward with the weight of the explosives strapped to his back. Sterne had the blasting caps and det cord, but they only weighed a couple of pounds.

Through the branches of the bushes Sterne could see little. He could tell they were twenty-five or thirty feet above the jungle floor and were looking into the branches of palm trees. Through gaps in the leaves he could see the ground, the sunlight throwing irregular patterns on the greens, browns, and blacks of the jungle floor. He thought he could see one of the SEALS crouching near a bush but wasn't sure whether it was a man or a shadow.

He inched his way upward then, along the split in the rock, sliding his feet carefully and moving his hands cautiously. The crack turned and began to climb at a sharp angle. Sterne studied it, saw that there was good cover along it, and eased himself upward so that his feet were braced on the crack. He stepped carefully, over Ross's hands, continuing the climb.

From the jungle he could hear the shouting back and forth, Tynan just making noise, trying to keep the enemy's attention on them, on the jungle floor. When the shouting stopped, Sterne halted momentarily, resting. He felt the sweat pop onto his forehead. He felt it tickling his sides and dripping down his chest making him itch. The palms of his hands were becoming slippery with it.

Above him he could see little except blue sky. He was so close to the cliff face that he couldn't see how much higher it was. The vegetation at the top blended with that from the rock, making it seem to extend almost forever. He took a deep breath and refused to look upward again. He just kept sliding his feet along the crack as it angled upward.

He came to a vertical split. There was a slight overlap, so that the crack was partially concealed. The inside was ragged, full of handholds and toeholds, and it seemed to run to the top of the cliff. Bushes and vines helped to hide it from the jungle floor.

Sterne worked his way around the side of the split and started to climb up the inside of it. As he moved along it, it widened and deepened, providing more and better cover. He scrambled upward and in seconds found himself at ground level. The crack opened into a circular pit nearly twenty feet in diameter. By crawling around the edge of it, he could move away from the edge of the cliff and stay concealed from anyone on the jungle floor below, or hiding in the jungle on the top of the cliff.

He reached back, grabbed Ross's hand, and helped him up. Then he crept along the rim of the depression until he came to a large bush. On his belly, he crawled out, along the ground, until he was hidden in the vegetation. He halted there, waiting, watching and listening. From the jungle floor he could hear Tynan shouting answers to the enemy commander. They seemed to be verbally sparing, jockeying for position.

Ross suddenly appeared beside him and asked, "We in the clear?"

"I think so," said Sterne. "I don't see or hear anyone up here with us."

"Now what?"

Sterne didn't answer right away. He pulled out his map. It was a sodden mess that was hard to read. He folded it over, stared at it, but couldn't find a reference to the cliff on it. The elevation lines were fairly close together, but they didn't give any indication of the cliff. To the east, about half a klick, the elevations seemed to spread out, which would mean a hillside rather than a cliff.

"Let's head over there," said Sterne.

"I'll follow you."

"Okay, but stay far enough behind me that if we do run into something, you might be able to back out of it."

"Got it."

For more than ten minutes, the man had not said a word. Tynan had, at first, been worried about it, afraid of what he might be planning, and then remembered the wall. It was to teach patience. It was a lesson that was hard for many to understand, especially those raised in a society where every waking moment had to be useful. Anyone who sat quietly, thinking, was considered to be wasting time. Something productive had to be done with every minute of every day.

Tynan smiled at that. Although he was only lying on the ground, partially concealed by a log, he was doing something useful. He was tying up the enemy's soldiers who were out there waiting for him to surrender. Tynan didn't have to do anything now that Sterne and Ross were gone. He was sure that they had reached the top of the cliff. If they hadn't, somehow Sterne would have let him know. Time was back on his side. Patience was again the key.

Boone, who was lying under the leafy part of a bush, crawled to his right so that he was near Tynan. "How long we going to wait here?"

"I think we've been here about long enough," said Tynan. "We'll withdraw to the cliff and then work our way east along it until we're clear."

"What about Hollinger?"

"I'm afraid the Animal will have to get himself out of his own mess." Tynan rolled to his side and glanced at his watch, thinking that everything was taking too much time. Way too much. "Alert the others. I'll take the point."

"Aye, aye, Skipper."

"American soldiers. I grow tired of this game. There is no need for it. Let us get together and talk about it. You are powerless. Why don't you surrender and end this quickly so we can get out of this heat?"

Tynan wasn't going to answer, but then he thought that the enemy commander might become suspicious if he didn't. He called out, "Back off and we'll head to the coast ourselves." To Boone he said, "I'm moving out in two minutes. Get the others ready to follow."

"Aye, aye."

"You know I cannot let you go, American soldiers," said the enemy commander; then, not waiting for Tynan's response: "Let us hike to the coast together."

"I will confer with my people," shouted Tynan, trying to buy some time.

"Hurry it up, American soldiers. We grow weary of this game and this place."

Tynan saw Boone and Jones moving toward him. With that, he began to crawl to the rear. He reached the base of the cliff. There was a space between it and the vegetation of the jungle floor, a trail along it, sprinkled with patches of sunlight. Tynan got to his feet and worked his way along it, trying to stay to the shadows.

It didn't take him long to reach the very edge of the enemy's thin line. In front of him Tynan could see a soldier crouched just inside the shadows cast by the trees and bushes of the jungle. The enemy was a white man who was not wearing the khaki of the local militia but a uniform that resembled the OD of Tynan's. From the insignia just barely visible, Tynan was sure that he was a Soviet soldier.

The soldier had to be the anchor of the enemy commander's position. There were two choices. One was to quietly kill the man and pass by him, and the other was to momentarily disable him. The problem with the second choice was that those momentarily disabled often recovered at the worst possible instant. The correct action was to permanently remove the Soviet. There might be international repercussions later, but the real problem was the Blackbird. Tynan had to make sure that it was destroyed, and the fact that the Soviets were there, surrounding him, virtually holding him prisoner, meant that the Soviets realized the importance of the plane.

Tynan held up a hand and signaled his men to cover. He slipped the sling of his AK-47 from his shoulder, dropped his pack, and shrugged himself free of his web gear. He didn't want anything rattling, or dragging, or catching on the local plant life. He rocked to his side, pointed at Boone, and then touched the ground near his equipment with his finger, telling Boone to move to that point.

He then began to crawl forward, moving one hand and placing it carefully among the fallen leaves, twigs, and debris on the jungle trail. He moved his foot, lifting himself off the ground slightly, creeping forward, almost like a jungle cat about to reach its prey. He got the rhythm going, hands and feet working together.

When the soldier turned toward him, as if searching the ground, Tynan froze. He dropped his eyes to the jungle trail so that he wouldn't communicate telepathically with the Soviet. Tynan wasn't sure that he believed in ESP, but he could see no reason to press his luck. When he glanced up and saw that the Soviet had turned his head, Tynan began to move again, quietly, carefully.

Tynan diverted slightly, moving from the trail closer to the cliff, until he was hidden behind a low bush made of tiny leaves and long thorns. He got to his hands and knees and worked his way around it until he was behind the Soviet soldier. Slowly, silently, he crept closer.

"American soldiers," the commander's voice suddenly shouted. "Why do you persist in this game? It is too hot and sticky to continue it."

The Soviet soldier seemed to snap awake at the sound of his commander's voice. He looked to the south, where his commander was hidden, staring into the jungle there. Once he glanced back where Tynan and his men were supposed to be, but then he settled down.

"Why do you no longer talk to me, American soldiers?" the Soviet asked.

Tynan felt that he was close enough. He slowly raised himself off his knees and rocked back so that he was on the balls of his feet, his fingers pressing lightly in the dirt of the jungle floor. He silently pulled his knife from the scabbard fastened to his boot, the razor-sharp edge of the blade pointed toward him. He hesitated for an instant and then sprang, his left hand reaching for the chin of the Soviet soldier. In one quick motion, Tynan dragged the man back, jamming his knee into the Soviet's spine, bending him backward, as he lifted the chin and sliced at the throat of the Russian.

As the blood washed over his hand Tynan pulled backward harder and plunged the knife into the man's chest, up under the breastbone, so that the blade pierced the heart and cut into one of the lungs, collapsing it. The man's feet shot out from under him, drumming on the soft earth. Tynan rocked back, dragging the body with him as he felt all the tension drain from the dead man. Tynan rolled the body to the right so that it landed facedown. He pushed it under a bush, trying to hide it but realizing that the dead soldier would not go unnoticed long during a real search.

Boone reached him then, carrying the equipment Tynan had left behind. He looked at the Soviet, saw the fresh blood staining Tynan's uniform and the blood-dripping knife he held. He raised an eyebrow in question.

Rather than answer, Tynan grabbed his web gear and slipped into it. He took his rifle, checked it, and then put on the safety. Without a word, he began to work his way along the cliff to the east.

From behind them they heard the enemy commander shout, "American soldiers. If you do not answer quickly, we shall have to come in there to get you."

12

The Soviet commander, Captain Vladimir Molodin, sat on the damp log, his elbows on his knees, and watched the American who crouched near him. Molodin didn't like using English, but the American refused to speak anything else. "Do you wish to speak to your friends?" he asked.

"You're doing just fine," responded Hollinger. "You don't need my help."

"If you will cooperate," countered Molodin, "we might get out of the jungle faster and you can return to your friends and your home."

Hollinger looked up at the Soviet. "Bullshit."

Molodin stared at him for a moment and then stood up. "American soldiers," he yelled. "It is time for things to end." He grinned at Hollinger. "Come out, or I will be forced to shoot your friend."

"That won't work." Hollinger grinned. "We don't play the hostage game. Ever."

"Then that is too bad for you," said Molodin, "because I will shoot you."

"Cut the crap, Comrade," said Hollinger. "You're not going to shoot me because of all the international problems it would create."

"Do not bet the family farm on it," said Molodin, smiling at his use of the Americanism.

One of the other Soviets appeared then. He stared at the big American sitting on the ground and then spoke to Molodin in rapid-fire Russian. "I think the Americans may have slipped away."

"What do you mean?"

"They have not answered your challenges for a while, and we can hear no movement from their positions. They may have retreated to the cliff and climbed it in some fashion or made their way through our lines."

Molodin spun so that he was facing the vegetation-shrouded cliff. "American soldiers, if you do not respond immediately, I will shoot your friend." He drew his pistol.

Hollinger jerked upright, staring at the weapon. He watched as the Soviet cocked it. He said calmly, "Now wait just a minute."

"Answer now, American soldiers, or I will shoot." When there was no response, he pulled the trigger. A single shot reverberated through the jungle.

Sterne stopped moving when he heard the sound of a shot drifting to him across the sea of the jungle. He turned, looking back toward the east, where it had come from, but could see nothing there. The sound had been faint. He wiped the sweat from his face and then waited for Ross.

"What d'you think?" asked Ross, catching up to him.

"Nothing. I think nothing. Now get back there." Sterne didn't wait for a response but began moving again, having turned to the south. They had descended from the plateau a klick from where they had climbed the cliff. It had been easy because the stone cliff had given way to a steep hill covered with trees and bushes. It looked as if part of the cliff had collapsed centuries earlier.

Once down, they had found a game trail and followed it for another klick until it disintegrated near a small pool of sparkling water. Sterne had stopped long enough to fill his nearly empty canteen, snapped it back onto his pistol belt, and then plunged into the jungle on the opposite side of the stream. The walking had become more difficult, but Sterne ignored that, moving as rapidly as the thick jungle would allow. The ground was gently rolling, giving them trouble as they had to climb the hills.

Thirty minutes after they heard the shot, Sterne stopped again, sure that he was now near the wreckage of the plane. He took a final look at his map and realized that he recognized nothing on it, but there weren't many landmarks he would have been able to see anyway. He waited for Ross and then waved him to the ground, signaling him to stay put while he, Sterne, explored the jungle around him.

He shed most of his equipment, leaving it near a giant palm where Ross could keep an eye on it. Carrying only his AK-47 and his pistol belt with his machete and canteen on it, he crept forward. At first there was nothing to see other than more jungle, but then he spotted something shiny lying in the dirt. He moved to it and recognized it as a piece of metal from the outer skin of the Blackbird. After wandering around the jungle all morning, he had managed to find his way back to the plane in fairly short order.

Before he could move, he heard voices, some of them speaking French and some of them speaking Russian. Sterne dropped to the ground and began to crawl forward. In seconds he was near the side of the plane, watching people seem to swarm over it. Many of them wore civilian clothes, some of them dressed like the great hunter in khaki safari jackets and bush hats with simulated animal hides around the crown. A few of the others, dressed in dark green uniforms, carried weapons, mainly AK-47s. There was a sprinkling of black men with the white. They wore the same khaki uniforms that Sterne had seen worn by the local militia the day before. The whole party seemed organized and official. Sterne felt that the local government was helping the people who were obviously Soviets examine the plane that even with its flat black paint and few identification markings was obviously of American design.

Sterne had no idea about Hollinger. All he knew for sure was that the plane hadn't been destroyed and the Soviets were studying it. He watched them working for a few minutes. It seemed that they had just arrived. They were proceeding slowly, as if afraid that it might have been booby-trapped. He counted three Russian soldiers with the civilians and thought there were ten local militia. He couldn't be sure, because, like the civilians, they kept moving around. Altogether, he thought there were at least thirty people crawling around the aircraft.

Sterne eased himself backward, then crept through the jungle until he came to Ross. He put his lips next to Ross's ear and said, "Thirty people, about half of them armed, at the plane. With surprise, we should be able to capture them."

Ross stared at him for a moment and then repeated, "Capture them?"

"Look, there are only three guys we have to worry about, and they were standing close together. We pop out of the jungle, armed, and order them to toss away the weapons. They do it or we shoot them. I don't think the locals will give us any real trouble."

"What about the civilians?"

"What about them?" asked Sterne. "They're civilians. Just like any other group of civilians. They're not going to attack into the barrels of blazing guns for the greater glory of Mother Russia. That done, I'll watch the soldiers and you can rig the plane."

"That's a lot of people, even if they are civilians, for one man to watch," said Ross.

"We could shoot them all, if that would make you happier," said Sterne.

"You know what I mean."

Sterne nodded. "Yeah. Look, give me ten minutes to get into place, then be ready. I'm going to step out of the jungle and order everyone to raise his hands. Anybody fucks with me, I'm going to shoot him. You make some noise from the other end as I come out and maybe we can surround them."

"It's not going to work," said Ross.

"I know that, but there's nothing I can do about it. We have to try before those fucking civilians learn everything there is to know about the plane."

"Good luck," said Ross.

"Ten minutes. Wait for me. You'll hear my voice."

"Got it."

Sterne rummaged through his gear, grabbed the spare magazines from it, his combat knife, and the grenade that he had sneaked out of the arms locker on the ship, just in case. He then crawled into the jungle, got cautiously to his feet, and, in a crouch, worked his way through the trees and around the thorny bushes until he was standing opposite the three Russian soldiers. He looked at his watch, saw that he had a little more than a minute, and began to ease toward the Soviets. Through the gaps in the foliage he could see them, sometimes just a shoulder or a leg or a belly and sometimes all of one of them.

Then there was a single tree separating them. Sterne hesitated and then stepped out. On the spur of the moment he fired a burst into the ground at the feet of the soldiers, then jerked his weapon up so that it was centered on the chest of the middle Soviet. In English he said, "Just drop them."

To his right he heard a noise and was tempted to glance toward it, but that would be the opening the Soviets wanted. He hoped that it was Ross and felt his back tingle as he waited for a bullet to strike it.

All three of the Soviets looked toward the sound and then, one by one, dropped the weapons they held.

Sterne motioned them back and, when they moved, used his foot to kick the rifles to the rear, away from the men.

A voice, male, old, came to him and demanded in English, "Just what are you doing?"

Sterne kept his eyes locked on the three soldiers. He didn't trust them in the least and realized he had made a mistake by not shooting them immediately. The problem was that the situation didn't allow him to just cut them down.

"Shut up," hissed Sterne. "Shut up and get your people over here."

Now he stepped back, putting more distance between himself and the Soviet soldiers. He was almost afraid to look anywhere except at the soldiers and wondered how he was supposed to watch thirty people by himself. Ross was right. It wasn't going to work.

"Ross!" he called. "Get them over here."

Out of the corner of his eye, he saw the others begin to approach. They filtered out of the depths of the jungle around him. Unconsciously, he took another step back. Two of the people stopped just at the edge of his vision, and Sterne fought off another temptation to look at them.

Then a couple of others appeared, walking toward the rear of the plane where Sterne held the soldiers. They didn't stop but kept coming, putting themselves between Sterne and the soldiers he was trying to cover.

"No!" he shouted, but it was too late.

Each of the soldiers leaped in a different direction. Sterne let his weapon follow the one in the center and fired twice, the rounds slamming into the man, throwing him to the ground. Blood spurted from the twin holes in the man's chest, one above each breast pocket. The burst crashed through the silence of the jungle, echoing back and forth until it sounded as if a platoon were shooting.

He spun, tracking another soldier who had reached the discarded weapons. Sterne fired once, the bullet catching the soldier in the middle of the forehead, smashing him to the ground in a loose-boned way that meant he was dead before he fell. The bullet hole was a neat, nearly bloodless wound, but the back of his head blew off, splattering the green of the jungle with red and gray.

The last of the soldiers turned to see Sterne pointing his weapon at him. He froze, his hand inches from his rifle. Slowly he turned so that he could look at his two dead comrades. Then he turned his attention back to Sterne.

There was a burst from the right and a piercing scream like tires on dry concrete.

"Ross?" demanded Sterne.

"I'm fine," Ross shouted back, his voice shaky. "The locals got a little feisty, but I put a stop to it. Three of them are down."

The authoritative voice that had come from the group of prisoners spoke again. "You men have no right to come in here and begin—"

"Shut up!" said Sterne. "I'm in no mood to debate the situation with you, so just shut up."

For a moment, Sterne didn't move or speak. Finally he said, "All right, I want everyone to sit down in front of me. Carefully. Then each of you will put your hands on top of your head and you will remain that way. Anyone moves, I'll be forced to shoot again. There are too many of you for anything else."

When no one moved right away, Sterne said, "You, with the rights, you tell these people what I want them to do, and tell them fast."

There was a rapid speech in Russian, followed by one in French. The people then began moving forward and sitting down. For the first time, Sterne noticed that there were two women in the group. One of them had blond hair and looked extremely frightened. He wanted to tell her not to worry, but, with two dead men lying practically at his feet, he knew that she would believe nothing he told her.

When the prisoners were all seated in front of him, and Ross was standing next to him, his AK-47 pointed at the group, Sterne risked a quick glance around. The plane was just as they had left it. A few access panels had been opened and one piece of equipment had been pried loose. It was sitting on the ground, under the SR-71.

The plane's nose rested on the dirt, the rear elevated by the trees it had crushed in the crash. The wings were bent and torn, and Sterne could see the damage done by shrapnel when the missile had exploded. He wanted to look in the cockpit, at the instrument panel, at the equipment in the various bays, but he didn't have the time. He knew that it would be dark in a few hours, and once that happened, there was no way for him to control all the prisoners. They had to be finished before nightfall.

"Okay, Ross," said Sterne. "Get with it."

Tynan was less than half a klick from the spot where he had killed the Soviet soldier when he heard the single pistol shot. His first reaction was to drop to the ground, but he realized that the shot came from a long distance. He hesitated, but there wasn't a second one.

Tynan moved off quickly, following the game trail that meandered along the base of the wall. After another couple of hundred meters, Tynan turned to the south, into the thick of the jungle. The undergrowth was thin at first, making travel easier than it had been in the morning but nowhere near as simple as it had been on the trail. Tynan kept the pace rapid, dodging around the obstacles, never hesitating. He glanced at his watch periodically, wondered how Sterne and Ross were doing, and kept waiting for the rumble that would tell him the plane had been destroyed.

The heat and humidity of the tropics no longer bothered Tynan. They had become a minor irritation. The Russians were now involved, and Tynan had killed one of them. He didn't know how their commander would react. The plane hadn't been destroyed yet, and Tynan didn't know how his own commanders would react to that. And he was doing all this on foreign soil, in a country that he had entered illegally. No, the heat and the humidity were the least of his problems.

He kept moving, shoving those thoughts out of his mind. He would worry about them later. Now he had to get back to the plane. He had to set up security so that Ross would have a chance to blow it. That done, he would want to see if he could get Hollinger away from the Soviets.

They had been moving for a good thirty minutes when they heard the first firing in the distance. Tynan dropped to one knee, his head down, using his ears like radar antennas, trying to determine the direction of the shooting. He glanced over his shoulder at Boone, who pointed to the southwest, where the plane should be. Tynan nodded his agreement.

Then, from the rear, near the face of the cliff, they heard more shooting. Tynan knew that it involved none of his men but then realized it meant the Soviet commander had tired of the game and was assaulting Tynan's old position. He didn't like the fact that the Soviet commander had ordered his men to open fire. It meant that the threat of an international incident did not worry the Soviets greatly.

Tynan got to his feet and looked at the men behind him. He said nothing to them, just raised a fist and pumped it twice in the infantryman's double-time signal. With that, he jogged off, no longer concerning himself with noise discipline or leaving a trail for the enemy to follow. Once again time had become a critical factor. He had to get back to the SR-71 before the Soviets did.

They kept up the quick pace for fifteen minutes, but then the jungle thickened again, the undergrowth becoming dense, slowing them. Tynan got out his machete and began hacking at the bushes and vines, swinging the machete almost like a baseball bat. Finally, his arms aching, the sweat pouring from his body, Tynan dropped to the jungle floor and wiped the sweat from his forehead. He checked his compass again, pulled out his soggy map that threatened to disintegrate if he didn't treat it gently, and then looked upward, toward the sky. The sun had long passed its nearly cloudless zenith and was beginning the rapid plunge to the western horizon.

Boone caught up to him and said, "You want me to take the point, Skipper?"

"Yeah," said Tynan, breathing heavily. "Why don't you take the point. Follow a compass heading of two-nine-five. I make it three klicks to the crash site. When we get close, we'll need to slow down and inch our way in quietly. We don't want to surprise anyone."

Boone took Tynan's machete and began to chop his way through the jungle. He had only gone about a hundred meters when the undergrowth thinned again. Boone stopped long enough to hand the machete back to Tynan and then asked, "You want me to stay on the point?"

"Yeah," said Tynan, "but be alert for anything out of the ordinary."

Jones joined the group then and said, "I think they're closing in on us."

"Christ, not again," said Boone.

"Makes sense," responded Tynan. "We've had to chop our way through this. They could just follow us through, gaining on us all the time."

"I think they're about a hundred meters back, but they're gaining."

"Boone, take off. Let's get moving."

Boone took a quick look at his compass, sighted on a large tree, and headed toward it. He maintained a steady pace, now worried about noise discipline. Twenty minutes later he slid to a stop.

Tynan came up beside him, but before he could speak, Boone pointed. There, just visible through the trees and bushes, Tynan could see twenty or twenty-five men, sitting on the ground, their hands on their heads. He moved forward slowly, quietly, until he could see that the black men were wearing the khaki uniforms of the local militia and the white men dressed for a safari. Then, watching them carefully, he saw Sterne.

"All right," he said to Boone and Jones. "Let's go help them and get the job done."

"Skipper," said Jones. "The enemy is closer now. I think they've almost caught up."

13

With the Soviet patrol pressing him from the rear, Tynan didn't have the luxury of delay. He would have liked to study the situation in front of him before blundering into it, but he had no time. He stood up and stepped around the tree so that he was now close to the Blackbird. With one hand, he waved both Jones and Boone onto the crash site so that they would be visible to the prisoners.

"We've arrived," said Tynan to announce himself.

He saw the barrel of Sterne's weapon waver slightly, but Sterne did not turn his head. He kept his attention focused on the prisoners, watching them steadily and waiting for them to make a move.

"Glad you could make it, Skipper," said Sterne.

"You can relax," said Tynan. "We've got the people here covered."

Sterne lowered his weapon and sighed. He wiped a sleeve across his forehead. "Wow," he said. "I didn't know watching people could be such a task."

"Where's Ross?" asked Tynan.

"Rigging the plane for destruction." Sterne turned and pointed toward the cockpit. "He was back over there somewhere a moment ago."

"You wait here and help Boone and Jones guard the prisoners." Tynan took a final look at the men seated there, saw that there were two women in the group and thought that something should be done for them. They should be moved somewhere, given something, but he really had no idea exactly what he should do. He decided that it was a misplaced sense of chivalry. They would just have to suffer with the rest.

He moved across the crash site to where the nose of the SR-71 had hit the ground, pushing up a slight rise of blackened earth. He saw a boot descend from one of the larger access bays under the belly of the plane. The toe was pointed down, as if feeling for the ground, and when it touched the earth, the other foot appeared. A second later Ross had climbed from the plane and was standing up.

"How much longer?" asked Tynan.

"Jesus!" said Ross. "Don't go sneaking up on people." He ducked under the plane and then came back to stand next to Tynan. "The Animal got a lot of the work done before the Soviets carted him off. These people didn't bother to remove the explosives, so most of them are in place."

"How long?"

"Another fifteen minutes," said Ross, thinking quickly. "Maybe less."

"Hurry it up. The other patrol is on our tail." Tynan glanced at the prisoners. "How far from here do we have to be when the plane goes up?"

"Half a klick."

"What's the absolute minimum?" asked Tynan.

"A hundred meters if we have some protection. Why?"

"Because I don't want to leave anything to chance. The Soviets are going to appear in a moment and we're going to have to finish the job under their noses."

"You want it command detonated?"

"That would be ideal."

"I'll see what I can do."

Then from the jungle came a shout. "American soldiers, this is doing you no good. Give it up."

"You've just lost time," Tynan told Ross. "Get it ready now."

"There is one other thing, Skipper. Some of the equipment from the plane is missing. I haven't found it around here. Did the pilots take anything with them?"

"I wasn't told of anything taken out by the pilots. Exactly what is missing?"

"Nothing big. Looks like a couple of the black boxes. There's a couple of gaps in the racks where the equipment is mounted."

"You try my patience, American soldiers," came the voice from the jungle. A voice that was becoming too familiar to Tynan and his men.

"We don't have time to worry about it anymore," Tynan told Ross as he looked into the jungle toward where he had heard the voice. "Ignore it. Get this thing ready to blow up. I'll buy us a little time."

"Aye, aye, Skipper."

Tynan ran back to Sterne. "Get these people on their feet and herd them to the south. Watch out for an ambush. The Soviets have arrived again."

"American soldiers—"

"I hear you," Tynan shouted back, irritated. "I also hold a couple of dozen of your people, so just back off right now. I don't want to hurt them."

"Skipper, I don't think we should attempt to move. They wouldn't have announced their presence unless they had us surrounded."

"Granted, except that is going to spread them thin. They were spread very thin at the cliff and they had less territory to cover."

"Aye, aye." Sterne yelled, "On your feet. Let's—"

"Quietly," snapped Tynan. "Quietly. We don't need to transmit our plans to the Soviets."

Boone and Jones began moving among the prisoners, forcing them to their feet. They formed them into a line and moved them to the far side of the plane so that they all stood close to one of the crumpled wings.

"American soldiers—"

Tynan interrupted again. "Here is the deal," he shouted. "You send in our man and I'll return yours to you."

"That hardly seems fair," said the man in the jungle. "You hold so many more of our people."

Tynan glanced at the group of civilians under the wing. He pointed to the women and said to Sterne, "Bring the women here." Then Tynan called to the man in the jungle, "I'm sending two of your people to you now. They will be entering the jungle."

There was no response. Tynan pointed at the women and snapped his fingers, signaling them forward. He gestured at the jungle, nodded, and said, "Go on."

The women stood there confused for a moment, staring first at Tynan and then at each other. One of them took a tenative step toward the jungle but seemed unsure of herself.

Tynan raised his voice again and yelled, "Call your people. They do not want to come to you."

For a moment nothing happened, and then the man in the jungle shouted in Russian, "Come ahead. You will be all right. One of my men will meet you."

Both women moved at once, glancing back at Tynan, watching him carefully. They entered the jungle, ducked around a large palm, and vanished from sight.

Tynan spun and said, "Move them out. Half a klick and find some cover."

At that moment Ross appeared. "That does it, Skipper. I can blow it as soon as everyone is in the clear."

"Okay. Take off. I'll be right behind you." He turned, saw the last of the men and Jones fade into the jungle. He called to the Soviet commander, "Now, where is my man?"

"You still hold so many more of mine, American soldier. If I return yours, I have no guarantee that you will return all of mine."

For the first time, Tynan believed that Hollinger might be dead, that the Soviet commander had actually shot him. Or maybe executed Hollinger after the Soviet soldier that Tynan had killed was found. There was nothing he could do about it now. Just play for a few minutes.

"I will consider the next move," called Tynan. He slipped backward, under the plane. He turned and ran into the jungle. In the distance he could see Ross as he moved. Tynan ran toward him and caught him near a huge tree that had bark that contained thousands of sharp spines.

"We far enough?" asked Tynan.

"I think so."

"Then blow it," said Tynan. "Blow it now."

Ross finished stringing his wire, cut it, and stripped the insulation from it. He wrapped the leads around the poles on the hand-held detonator and then crouched behind the giant tree. He looked up at Tynan and said, "Take cover."

Tynan flattened himself on the ground behind the tree, his hands over his ears.

"Fire in the hole!" screamed Ross. He hesitated, heard his voice echo, and yelled it again. Then, leaning as close to the tree as he dared because of the thorns, Ross spun the crank once, twice, three times to generate the electrical pulse that would detonate the explosives.

Tynan waited, and when he heard nothing he glanced at Ross, who had rolled to his stomach. He was going to speak when he heard the first of the explosions, a mighty crash that shook the jungle and vibrated the ground. There was a second and a third, and then a final massive explosion that sounded as if the entire earth had erupted. Debris began to rain down, showering through the trees. Tynan felt tiny pieces hitting around him. They were bits of dirt, rock, and wood. A few pieces of metal landed near his hand. He looked at them, knew they were from the plane, and wondered if the Soviets would be able to pick up enough of them to give them a clue about the composition of the alloy. He decided not to worry about it.

"That's it," said Ross. "The whole thing has gone up."

"Okay," said Tynan, getting to his feet. He wanted to run to Sterne and the others so that they could get out, but he knew there was one thing left to do. He had to make sure that the plane was gone, that a large part of it hadn't somehow escaped destruction. He pointed at Ross and said, "You join the others, I'll be there in a couple of minutes."

Ross got to his feet and ran into the jungle. Tynan worked his way back toward the crash site, but he hadn't gone far when he realized that the plane had been destroyed. Through the trees, many of them now standing at bizarre angles, their leaves stripped from them, he could see clouds of dust. He moved closer, saw trees that were little more than trunks, trees that had been cut in two, stumps that had been trees, and

then he saw the crater. Caught a glimpse of it through
the smoke and dust that drifted over the crash site.
There was nothing left of the SR-71 except the tiny
bits that were now scattered over a couple of klicks
of territory.

That was enough for him to confirm the destruction
of the plane. He whirled and ran back into the jungle,
detouring to the east. He found his men, the prisoners
scattered around them, all lying on their stomachs, as
if waiting for another explosion.

"Now what?" asked Sterne.

"Now we get out of here. Leave the prisoners and
head for the beach."

"What about the Animal? We can't leave him with
the Soviets. They'll kill him."

"We don't know that he's still alive," said Tynan.

"But we still can't leave him."

The sudden explosion had surprised Molodin. The
concussion had knocked him to the ground. He had
rolled over, wrapped his arms around his head, and
waited to die. Debris from the plane struck the earth
around him, fragments of the trees hit him in the back,
and bits of earth impacted near him. To his right,
Viktor Krothov lay with a splinter the size of a baseball bat through his chest. Grigori Kudira, who was a
hell of a sergeant major but not much of a medic, tried
to pull the wood from the body of the executive officer. Kudira was bleeding from his nose and ears; he
had been closer to the explosion than anyone else.

Slowly, unsteadily, Molodin got to his feet. To his
left he saw both the women. They had been thrown
to the ground by the force of the detonation. One was
doubled up, her mouth working rapidly as she tried
to suck in air. The other was shaking her head, her
long black hair streaked with dirt.

Molodin took a step and then stopped. He turned. Hollinger was getting to his hands and knees, but there was a grin on his face. Quietly he said, "Game. Set. And match."

"What does that mean?"

"It means the game is over and we have won. The plane no longer exists."

"But I still hold you captive."

"That's right, and my skipper holds a bunch of your people. But so what? This was about the airplane and not people. You might as well let me go now."

Molodin looked at the body of his executive officer. He thought about his soldier who had died so quietly at the base of the cliff. And he thought about the two soldiers who had been killed at the plane. The women had told him about their deaths. Four of his men dead and more of them injured. It was not something that he could let go of. There was more to be done, if it was only capturing the other Americans and taking them to Moscow to stand trial for international crimes.

He shook his head at the American and went over to help the women to their feet. The blonde had a bruise on the side of her face but didn't look badly hurt. In Russian, he asked her about her treatment after the Americans had captured her. She told him that they really had done nothing other than hold an automatic weapon on them. They had been left alone, hadn't even been searched, and just told to keep their hands on their heads. She had been scared for the first few moments, but then it became apparent that the Americans weren't going to hurt any of them if they did as they were told.

"Were the two men shot for failing to obey?" asked Molodin.

"No. They had been trying to reach their weapons. The American didn't hesitate and he didn't shoot the last of the soldiers, even though that man was also reaching for a weapon. But he hadn't gotten to it and had stopped moving.''

Molodin nodded. He left them to check on the rest of his men. No one had been badly hurt by the explosion. That Krothov died was one of those strange coincidences. If he had been standing six inches to the right, the shard would have missed him. His death could be called accidental.

In fact, the death of the two soldiers at the plane could be called accidental. If they hadn't gotten a case of the fatal stupids, they would still be alive. The only death that could be classed as premeditated was that of the soldier at the cliff. He had been stalked and killed.

Molodin realized that if the situation had been reversed, he would have done the same thing. He would have killed the soldier in the way. Still, there were too many dead Soviet soldiers just to let it go.

"You might as well free me," repeated Hollinger. "You gain nothing by holding on to me."

"You think that your comrades will leave you here?" asked Molodin.

"They have completed their mission. They will now exfiltrate even if I don't join them. Those are their orders."

"I am sorry, but I do not believe you. I think they will try to rescue you. This is not over yet."

14

Tynan looked at the men lying on the ground in front of him. There was no way that he could both guard them and rescue Hollinger, but he didn't want to set them free either. Then he realized that the majority of the people there were civilians. They would be of no value to the Soviet commander.

To Sterne, he said, "Separate the blacks from the Soviets and chase the blacks into the jungle. The move of the hour would probably be to shoot the last Soviet soldier, but he's done nothing other than get himself captured."

"Just chase the blacks away?" asked Sterne.

"That's right. Don't let them have any weapons and don't give them any food. Just get them the hell out of here. I don't want to do anything else to antagonize the local government. We've done enough already."

Sterne moved among the men, dragging the blacks to their feet, herding them away from the rest of the prisoners. When he had them at the rear of the group, he gestured at the jungle, waved, and yelled, "Go!"

Just as the Soviet women had done, the black men stood there looking at him. Again he yelled, "Go!" and then added, "You're free to leave. Get out."

Finally Boone moved to the group and yelled at them in broken, almost forgotten high school French. He told them to leave, to run away.

And just as the Soviet women had done, the men hesitated. Then one of them slipped from the group and fled into the jungle. Two or three of the others watched him. They saw the Americans make no attempt to catch him. Almost as one, the rest of the men ran into the trees.

The task completed, Sterne walked back to Tynan. "What'll we do with the Soviets?"

"That's a good question," said Tynan. "I suppose we keep them lying on the ground, tell them to bury their faces, and then just slip away."

"When they find we're gone, they're going to split. Right back to the main unit."

"That won't matter. They won't be able to go right to it. They'll mill around here for a little while, giving us a chance to find the Soviets and see if we can get the Animal."

"How soon?" asked Sterne.

"Just as soon as you tell Boone and Jones and Ross. Then we're on our way."

"Aye, aye, Skipper."

Tynan watched Sterne move to Jones and whisper to him. Tynan sat down on the ground. He looked up into the sky where there were clouds building, but they were white, fluffy clouds that didn't promise rain or relief from the heat. Tynan took out his canteen and shook it. There was only a little water in the bottom of it, and that would be warm bordering on hot. It would be very easy to drink it all in one spasmodic gulp. Then there would be no more water until after dark, after they had freed Hollinger and were fleeing through the jungle.

Using his sleeve, Tynan wiped his face. He was covered with sweat. The air was heavy with moisture, making it hard to breathe. The tropics in Africa were somehow worse than those of Asia. Tynan wondered if the problem was pyschological. In Asia he had had more control over the situation. Here he was reacting to it. Maybe that made the weather seem hotter and wetter. He wished that the sun would disappear for an hour or so.

"Prisoners are ready," Sterne reported.

"All right. Here's what we do. You take the point back to where the plane crashed. I'll bring up the rear. You get close, circle to the west, and then cut back. We'll have to maintain tight noise discipline if this is going to work. Once we're close, we'll try to get the drop on them."

Tynan watched Sterne slip to the right and then into the trees. Boone, then Ross, and finally Jones followed him. Tynan stood at the edge of the group, watching the prisoners. When one of them looked up at him, he fired a burst in the air and ordered, "Keep your heads down."

He then spun and ran after the rest of his men. He saw Jones in front of him and slowed. He let Jones stay about five, six meters in front of him. Like the others, he moved carefully, avoiding the dead leaves on the ground, although everything was so damp that Tynan thought it impossible to rustle leaves.

It didn't take them long to get back to the crash site. Sterne detoured around it, disappeared into the jungle again. Moments later, Tynan saw him crouching behind the trunk of a tree that had tried to fall, but its branches had gotten tangled with two others and it was slanted at a forty-five-degree angle.

Tynan slipped to the ground beside him. Sterne touched his shoulder and pointed, showing him where

Boone, Jones, and Ross now hid. Then he pointed to the front where it seemed that the Soviets were waiting.

Tynan nodded. He hesitated, his eyes on the jungle. He listened carefully but heard only the sounds of the animals as they screamed at one another or fled some small terror. Tynan got down and began to crawl forward, under the trunk of the fallen tree. He crept around a bush, listening, watching, and searching.

He hadn't gone far when he heard someone move to his left. Tynan froze and slowly turned his head. In the patterns formed by the late-afternoon sunlight and the leaves of the trees and bushes, Tynan could see a man in a dark green uniform. The man was standing next to a palm tree, one arm on the trunk. His rifle was slung as if he didn't expect trouble.

The last thing Tynan wanted to do was kill another Soviet soldier. But, just like the last time, there was no way to bypass the man without putting everyone else in jeopardy. Tynan waited until the man turned and was watching the jungle to the west. Then he began to creep toward him. As he approached, Tynan slipped off the safety of his rifle, just in case, but when he was only five feet from the man, Tynan knew that he would not have to shoot. Tynan started to get up, saw the man begin to turn, and froze. The man seemed to stare straight at him, and Tynan wondered why he didn't shout a warning. Instead, he moved toward Tynan, reaching out as if puzzled by what he saw.

Suddenly Tynan sprang forward. The soldier straightened instinctively. Tynan brought the butt of his AK around, striking the man on the point of the chin. His head snapped back and he staggered to the rear, taking a single step as he collapsed. Tynan's left hand shot out, trying to catch the falling soldier, but he missed. They was only a little noise as the man dropped onto a bush, crushing it.

Sterne was there immediately, whispering in Tynan's ear, "What'll we do with him?"

"Leave him. Have Ross watch him. We'll want someone covering our retreat anyway."

Tynan began moving forward again, hugging the ground. His rifle was cradled in his arms. His nerves sang with tension. He was tired, his eyes burning with a lack of sleep. He was sweating. He hadn't eaten anything for nearly twelve hours, but he didn't notice that. All he could do was concentrate on the task of crawling silently through the jungle.

He stopped near the trunk of a medium-sized palm at the edge of a small clearing. He peeked around it and saw three Soviet soldiers sitting there, their backs to him. In front of them was Hollinger, sitting on the ground, his hands shoved in the pockets of his fatigues. To one side were the two women Tynan had freed earlier. A single body, covered with some kind of green plastic tarp, was near a tree. A radio was sitting on a log, and Tynan could hear the quiet buzz of the carrier wave. A tiny red light glowed in the middle of the panel.

Tynan turned his head and saw Sterne stop just under a large bush. Near him was Jones. Although he couldn't see him, Tynan knew that Boone would be close by too. Again Tynan checked the safety on his weapon, making sure that it was off. Still he hesitated, waiting to see if anyone joined the Soviets, aware that he had left nearly two dozen prisoners behind and they could arrive at any moment.

Tynan saw Sterne staring at him. He held up a hand, telling Sterne to be patient. Then, slowly, using the tree for cover, Tynan got to his knees and finally to his feet. He saw Sterne move backward so that he was in the shadow of the bush. Without another thought, Tynan stepped into the clearing and yelled, "Hollinger, drop. Everyone freeze."

"Skipper, it's a trap," yelled Hollinger, trying to get to his feet.

There was a burst of fire that slammed into the tree near Tynan's head. Tynan fell to the ground and rolled to the right, firing. The bullets hit the radio, shoving it over. It sputtered, was silent, and then belched sparks.

The three men who had been facing away from him had seemed to disappear when Tynan yelled. They had fallen forward, rolling under the cover of a couple of logs cut down and placed there for protection.

Hollinger scrambled to his feet, trying to get out of the center of the clearing. He was leaping a small bush when the first shot was fired by the Soviets. It caught him in the shoulder and spun him around. He staggered, fell to his knees, and tried to get to his feet again. The second shot hit him in the face, snapping his head back. He jerked over, falling to his back, his face a crimson mask.

From the left, where Sterne had been, came a sustained burst of AK fire. The rounds kicked up dirt around the log barricade. It stripped the bark from it and concealed it behind a tiny cloud of dirt. From the inside came a shriek of pain as one of the bullets found its mark.

Tynan dived backward, landing near the tree. He crawled around it and saw one of the Soviets running toward the crash site. Tynan aimed and squeezed the trigger for a five-shot burst. The rounds stitched their way from the man's shoulder to the opposite hip, the blood blossoming quickly, staining his clothes. He pitched forward on his face. He didn't put his hands out to break the fall; he just slammed into the ground, rolled once, and lay still, his weapon near his outstretched hand.

All around him the firing began, with everyone using AK-47s, so that Tynan couldn't identify the hiding places of his own men. He worked his way to the right, keeping down, trying to outflank the log barricade where the three soldiers hid.

Then he saw Boone appear in the clearing, firing his weapon from the hip, pouring rounds into the logs. He was screaming at the top of his voice, his words running together unintelligibly. He ran to Hollinger's body, grabbed the shoulder, and began dragging it back the way he had come.

The firing increased in intensity. Tynan could see the ground near Boone's feet churning with the incoming fire. The leaves of the bushes behind shredded in tiny green explosions, the bits drifting to the earth. Tynan saw the muzzle flash of one of the enemy weapons and turned his own AK on it, hosing down the bushes and trees near it.

The others did the same. Sterne suddenly appeared, as if trying to draw the fire away from Boone. He, too, was shouting. He kept pouring fire into the Soviet positions until his weapon was empty. Then he reached into his pocket for his hand grenade, but, unlike John Wayne, Sterne did not pull the pin with his teeth. He looped it over his trigger finger, jerked the pin free, and tossed the grenade as far as he could into the trees.

There was an explosion a second later, but it was so deep in the jungle that no one saw it. They heard it, heard the shrapnel from it whir through the clearing, and heard the dirt rain back to the ground.

Tynan realized that the whole point of the exercise was to get Hollinger out. Boone had done that. Tynan crawled back to the tree. He saw Sterne stagger then, a round seeming to pass through his shoulder. That seemed to enrage Sterne. His face changed to a mask of rage and pain. He no longer aimed his weapon. He held the trigger down, spraying rounds throughout the jungle clearing.

From nowhere Jones appeared and grabbed Sterne by the back of the belt. He jerked him rearward as Sterne's weapon stopped firing, the bolt locked back by the empty magazine.

Now Tynan was on his feet, moving away from the clearing. He circled around and came to where Boone was crouched over the body of Hollinger. Tynan leaped forward and put a hand on Hollinger's throat. There was no pulse.

Over the sound of the shooting Tynan yelled, "The Animal's dead. We've got to get out now."

The firing from the Soviet camp seemed to swell until it was a continuous roar, the individual shots blending into a single noise like that of a buzz saw. The trees, the bushes, the ground around them seemed to vibrate with the impacts of the 7.62mm rounds.

"Fall back," ordered Tynan. "Fall back."

He started to move, saw that Boone seemed to be stunned, and reached out, grabbing him. He jerked on his shoulder, spinning the man so that he faced to the rear.

"Get out of here," he ordered.

Boone seemed not to understand for the moment. His eyes were fixed on Hollinger's body. Tynan gave him a shove, and Boone began to run through the jungle. Tynan shot a final glance at Hollinger. There was very little blood on his uniform. Most of it came from the wound in the face, the blood soaking into the ground under his head.

He saw one of the three Soviets who had been hiding under the logs stand. He sighted on him and fired again and again, single shot. Each impact of the bullet on the enemy's body made Tynan feel more powerful. He watched as the Soviet dropped his own weapon and clawed at his chest as if to remove a burning ember. He didn't fall for a moment, too dazed to realize what was happening to him. Tynan pumped round after round into him, smashing one of his legs, an arm, breaking both his hands. Finally, as if the wounds had become too much, too severe, the soldier collapsed backward, rolling to his stomach, suddenly screaming in pain.

With that, Tynan turned to run. He saw Jones in front of him, heading to the west, toward the coast where they could be picked up. Behind him the firing seemed to be tapering. The Soviets were no longer just pumping out rounds but were trying to fire at the fleeing SEALS.

Tynan came to the unconscious Soviet soldier. He was slightly surprised that Ross hadn't slit his throat when the shooting started, but glad that he hadn't. Tynan hesitated long enough to consider putting a bullet into the man's head, but he realized that he didn't have the stomach to murder someone like that. He could sneak up behind him and cut his throat because the man hadn't been alert enough or smart enough to hear him, but he couldn't shoot someone who was basically helpless.

Instead, he spun and emptied his magazine in the direction of the Soviets. He hit the release and let the clip fall free. He searched the unconscious man, found his spare ammunition, and stole it, jamming one of the magazines into his own weapon. That was the advantage of carrying the same weapons as the enemy. You could rearm from them.

Then he began to run. He followed the path left by his men. Periodically, in the distance, he would catch a glimpse of one of them. He hurried his pace, trying to catch them as they put distance between themselves and the Soviets. Now all he had to do was reach the coast. Reach the coast and have Jones use the radio they had packed in to make contact with their ship, which should have moved back into the territorial waters of the local country.

Behind him he heard the shooting end as the Soviets discovered that he and his men had abandoned the fight in much the same way that the VC eluded the Americans in South Vietnam, fading into the jungle at the first opportunity. The Soviets, because they were giving chase, had to proceed cautiously, always waiting for the ambush that Tynan didn't plan on laying.

He caught up to his men near a narrow stream that knifed through some of the thickest of the jungle. Sterne was on his stomach, his head under the water momentarily, trying to cool off and to get a drink. Ross was on his knees beside him, using cupped hands to scoop up water and bring it to his lips. Jones was facing the way they had just come, his weapon ready.

"Get on the horn," Tynan ordered him, "and tell the ship that we're on the way out. And tell them Kilimanjaro."

"Kilimanjaro?" repeated Jones. His breath was coming in spasms as he tried to recover from the run.

"Code to tell them that the plane is destroyed," Tynan explained. He then slipped to the ground, facing to the rear, watching and listening, trying to hear over the pounding of his own heart and the rasping of his own breath in his throat. He suddenly felt hot, as if he had a fever, and the sweat began to pour from him.

"Sterne," he said. "Downstream. A hundred meters, maybe two hundred, until you can find a good place for us to reenter the jungle."

Sterne scrubbed at his face and nodded. He knew that Tynan was trying to throw off the pursuit. By sticking to the streambed they could conceal their footprints, and by carefully reentering the jungle they might lose their trackers altogether. If the pursuit was hasty and they left no obvious signs, the Soviets might follow the stream a long way before they realized that the Americans had given them the slip.

Molodin stood in the center of the clearing and looked at the damage. The trap had backfired. The American had sacrificed himself to save his friends. It was the last thing that Molodin had expected from one of the capitalist pigs. Soviet doctrine had taught him that the Americans were weak, were soft, and cared about nothing except ways to increase their personal wealth. The captive American, knowing that he would be shot the moment he opened his mouth, had willingly given up his life. It was an important lesson for Molodin. He would not make the same mistake again.

Pankovski, one of the privates, was now tending to the wounded. There weren't many. The Americans had proven to be crack shots too. They had seemed to hit everyone they aimed at and made sure of the kill. A second lesson.

The major stepped up behind him and said in French, "We seem to have failed."

Molodin's first instinct was to slap the huge black man. His second was to accept the fact of his words. They had failed. They had failed to secure the plane. They had failed to capture the Americans, although they had the one body, for whatever propaganda usefulness it might have. These were failures that wouldn't be viewed with kindness in Moscow.

"It strikes me," said the major, "that we still have a chance to capture the Americans. They do not have transport. We do."

"Yes," agreed Molodin. "We have transport."

"And it strikes me," said the major, "that the Americans will have to head for the coast. We can easily beat them to the coast and be waiting for them."

Molodin grinned. "Yes. And you have soldiers to help us capture these Americans."

"Of course. These barbarians have entered my country illegally, engaged in warlike activities, killed some of my own men, killed some of yours, and destroyed equipment that belonged to my government. Well, equipment that became ours when it crashed here."

"Can you get the helicopter in here to pick us up?" asked Molodin.

"The orders have already been given. And there will be soldiers to meet us on the beach."

"So we will not chase the Americans through the jungle but leap over them and wait for them on the beach. I like this plan," said Molodin. "I like it very much."

15

Sterne led them rapidly down the streambed. He was running, his feet splashing the shallow water. He was dodging around the rocks that had tumbled into the stream, leaping over the trees that had fallen into it, and avoiding the sandy pits that provided poor footing. He moved rapidly, unconcerned about the noise he was making, trying only to put distance between himself and the Soviet troops he thought would be following.

Tynan brought up the rear. He had held back after the others had finished drinking their fill, wanting to make sure that the Soviets hadn't gotten too close to them. On the bank he saw a couple of dark spots of blood. He knew that Sterne had been wounded in the fight, although Sterne hadn't complained about the injury yet. It meant that the wound wasn't bad and that Sterne was more concerned about getting out of Africa as quickly as possible.

For a stream through the tropics, the water was remarkably cool. Tynan, as he plunged on, felt refreshed. The heat and humidity of the late afternoon vanished in a cloud of cool water. He had washed his face in it, had drunk it, and now was running through it. This might be the incentive to get his men moving with more enthusiasm. It was surprising what could provide inspiration in the field. Cold water in a hot climate was one of them.

Running through water that was, at times, knee deep was easy, compared with chopping through thick jungle. Tynan slowed down, stopped, and listened, but the only sounds he heard were the animals in the treetops and his men splashing along the stream. The Soviet pursuit seemed to have been lost in the distance.

Tynan, having caught his breath, continued on more slowly, still listening for the Soviets. Two hundred meters along, after a turn in the stream that was lined with stone and as the bed of the stream turned to rock, he came to his men. Sterne had dropped over a small waterfall to the shallow stream below them. He was moving away, the sound of his feet lost in the roar of the waterfall.

Ross was next, working his way down the side of the falls, using as toeholds and handholds the protruding rock and the roots of trees that had forced their way through cracks. He reached the bottom and began to walk, slowly, in the direction that Sterne had taken.

"Water's not going to be good for the radio," said Jones as Tynan approached.

"Can't be helped," said Tynan. "Do what you can."

"In this environment, I wouldn't count on it drying very fast. Rust is more likely."

"A little water shouldn't hurt it," said Tynan. "These things are designed to be used outside, in the humidity and rain and weather."

Jones grinned at his skipper. "Sure. And if my grandmother had wheels she'd be a tea cart."

"You don't trust the environmental testing done by the manufacturer?" asked Tynan.

Jones just shook his head as if Tynan had said something incredibly stupid. He snorted and responded, ''Putting a radio in a box to pretend it's undergoing environmental stress is not the same as carrying it in the field.''

''Let's get going,'' said Tynan. The radio was just one more thing to worry about, and right then he had all the things he cared to worry about.

He watched Jones climb down, being careful of the tiny cloud of mist at the base of the fall. Jones moved along the stone bank until he was well away from the mist and then entered the water, following the path of Sterne.

When Jones was clear, Tynan followed his route. Once he slipped, but he grabbed a thick root that had looped back on itself and regained his balance. He reached the lower level and ran after his men, still wondering what in the hell the Soviets were doing. If they had killed as many of his men as he had killed of theirs, he would be chasing them. Especially if he were a Soviet. The Soviets punished failure with a firing squad. Tynan might be reprimanded, might be thrown out of the service, or might be given a dead-end job, but at least he wouldn't be shot for failing.

The stream cut back to the east, and Tynan found his men grouped on an outcropping of rock, drying themselves in the fading sunlight. He was concerned about their lack of security, but there had been no sign of pursuit and, since he was bringing up the rear, there was no reason to suspect that the Soviets were close.

''Good place to enter the jungle,'' said Sterne. ''Rock extends into the trees a little ways, so that you have to leave the streambed to see it. We wouldn't leave any sign until we're in the trees, and the bad guys might miss it. It's sure to slow them down some.''

"Skipper," said Ross." We need to rest. Get something to eat."

"Not yet. We'll want to make some time while we still have the sun. When it's dark we'll stop long enough to eat before heading on. I want to reach the beach before sunup tomorrow."

Sterne didn't wait for anything more. He dropped from his rock and vanished into the jungle. Ross followed him immediately, as did Jones and then Boone. Tynan hesitated again, listening, but now even the sounds of the animals scrambling about had disappeared. He thought he could still hear in the distance the water cascading over the miniature falls, but he couldn't be sure about that. Still there was no indication that the Soviets were behind him.

Not far into the jungle, Tynan found his men had halted again. Sterne, seeing him, came forward.

"Skipper, I've located a trail. Heads more or less to the west."

"Another game trail?"

"I don't think so. This one is too wide, and it looks like some of the trees and bushes have been chopped back. You think we should use it?"

Tynan rubbed a hand over his face. He could feel the stubble of his beard and the dirt from the jungle. Using a trail in Vietnam invited ambush. Invited sudden death. But this was not Vietnam, and the Soviets already knew that Tynan and his men were in-country. But the Soviets were somewhere behind them and had no idea of the escape route. Hell, even Tynan didn't know the escape route. He was making it all up as he went along. The trail would increase their speed, putting them on the Atlantic coast that much faster.

"Okay," he said. "We use the trail, but we spread way out. Just keep the man in front of you in sight."

"Aye, aye."

"And, Sterne, we need to make some time. It's probably a good twenty miles to the coast."

"Skipper," said Jones, "if we're heading for the coast for exfiltration, then we can ditch a lot of our equipment."

For a moment, Tynan thought about it. Without the heavy packs and web gear they would be able to travel farther, but Tynan was afraid of throwing away equipment, because there was no way of knowing what might come in handy later. The point was that they had to make time.

"Toss everything here except ammo, food, and water," he ordered them.

Tynan watched as the men stripped their packs, leaving behind equipment they now considered useless. They threw their poncho liners, clean socks, towels, packs of cigarettes, some of the C rations such as the canned bread and jelly into the pile. Tynan was going to tell them to burn it and then decided against it. If the Soviets were following, they would already know the path Tynan was using, and if they weren't, the equipment might be useful to the natives. This wasn't Vietnam where you left nothing for the VC.

"Okay, Sterne, take off."

Sterne began to lope down the trail, his weapon held at the ready. His pace was quick because he wasn't worried about booby traps or ambushes. He would run into neither in the jungles of Africa. Those were fears left in Vietnam.

Tynan watched as his men fell in behind Sterne. Tynan joined in, again bringing up the rear and again worried because there was no indication that the Soviets were in pursuit. He couldn't believe that the Soviet leader would give up so easily, or that they would be so poor in the jungle that they wouldn't make an effort to follow.

That thought kept nagging at Tynan as he ran down the trail, leaping over obstacles. He slowed to a jog once or twice, almost as if the slower pace allowed him to rest, then speeded up as he began losing sight of Jones in the distance. He ran until the heat of the jungle threatened to overwhelm him and his breath was coming in fiery, ragged gasps that burned his throat and lungs. He ran until his heart pounded, his ears rang, and his side ached. And then he ran some more, slowing a little until the hitch in his side evaporated. He ran as the sweat poured from him, stinging his eyes and soaking his clothes.

He ran as the sun dropped to the horizon and the light faded from the jungle. He ran as darkness swallowed everything around him. He ran until the trail seemed to disintegrate and the jungle vegetation rose up, slowing him.

He found Sterne crouched at the side of the vanishing trail, his arm against the trunk of a palm tree, his head resting against his arm. He was breathing rapidly. He could see neither Jones nor Ross, but he could hear them breathing hard, somewhere close by.

"We'll take a break," said Tynan. "A break. Eat. And drink. Then we'll move on." He shot a glance at Sterne, saw the bullet hole in his uniform that was surrounded by a dried bloodstain. Tynan pointed at Boone. "Why don't you take a look at Sterne and see how badly hurt he is."

"Aye, aye, Skipper." Boone moved across the trail, pushed Sterne's hands out of the way, and used his knife to cut the fatigue jacket. He turned so that he could speak to Tynan. "Doesn't look bad, Skipper. Little iodine and a Band-Aid should take care of it."

"Do it, then," said Tynan. He moved the men into the trees, away from what was left of the trail, and told them to eat something. Then he sat down, his

back to a large tree, and ate the last of the C rations
that he carried. When he finished the meal, a single
can of boned chicken for which he didn't even have
salt, he buried the cans under a foot of soft jungle
soil. He leaned back, closed his eyes, and let his mind
go. He didn't want to think about the mission, or
Hollinger, or the Blackbird, or even Wheeler sitting
in his air-conditioned office in London. He wanted to
concentrate on Bobbi, wondering if he should be angry
with her for agreeing to help the CIA talk him into
the mission, or be glad that she had wanted to see him
enough that she would take the assignment, even one
so underhanded.

But, although he tried to concentrate on Bobbi, the
Soviet leader kept intruding. Tynan hadn't liked the
way the man kept yelling at the American soldiers, or
the smug way in which he thought he could influence
them. The Soviet had underestimated the American
resolve every step of the way. Tynan and his men had
surprised the Soviet by being where they were, by
fighting their way clear, and by escaping.

Finally the weakness caused by the long run seemed
to wear off. Tynan's breathing had returned to normal
and, although he was hot, he was no longer sweating
heavily. Blackness had wrapped everything around. It
was time to get moving, even though there was still
no indication that the Soviets were on the trail, following them.

Tynan stood and moved toward Sterne. He found
the man nearly asleep, a can of boned turkey in one
hand and a white plastic spoon in the other. Ants were
swarming over the top of the turkey, looking like pep-
per that moved.

"Time to go," said Tynan quietly.

Sterne jerked once, as if waking, and then scrambled to his feet, annoyed with himself. "Aye, aye," he said.

"To the west. Use your compass," said Tynan.

"What kind of pace?"

"As fast as you can without risking injury. We've got eight hours to make it to the beach."

Together they told Ross and Jones that they were moving out. Sterne went ahead, his rifle slung and his compass in his hand. He had used Tynan's machete to chop a walking stick. Sterne had thrown away his machete when they had thrown away most of their equipment.

Now the pace was through a jungle that had little undergrowth. The pace ate up the distance, moving them closer to the coast and the ship. Each of them grew excited at the thought because it meant the ordeal of the last few days was nearly over. Each had his own thoughts about the first thing he would do when he set foot on the ship. The heat and danger of the jungle seemed to disappear as they rolled up the klicks, getting ever closer to retrieval.

Finally, in the distance, they could hear the rumble of the surf as it smashed into the coastline. Sterne threw his walking stick away so that he could run forward down the beach and leap into the sea. But Tynan had spent so much time teaching them discipline that Sterne resisted the temptation to enter the water. The worst time for a patrol was the few minutes before they arrived at their destination, because no one was alert anymore. They all figured that if anything was going to happen, it would have happened by then.

Tynan then ran forward, past both Jones and Ross, and caught Sterne before he could reach the end of the jungle. He touched his shoulder and said, "Hold it."

Sterne stopped and said, in a voice that was too loud, "Why stop now?"

Gesturing for him to get down, Tynan said, "I have a bad feeling about this. The Soviets haven't been yapping at our heels as I would expect. Let's just scope the situation before we go running out onto the beach."

Now Sterne was worried. He nodded.

Boone, Ross, and Jones caught up to them. Tynan whispered, "Try for radio contact. Let them know we're at the beach but that we're scoping things out."

"Aye, aye," said Jones. He slipped the radio from his back and turned to adjust it. He attached the earpiece and cranked in the ship's frequency. Quietly he whispered into the mike.

Tynan turned his attention back to the beach. He pointed right and left and then at two of his men, and watched as Boone and Sterne moved in opposite directions along the edge of the jungle. Tynan inched forward, suddenly worried about noise discipline. He eased himself to the ground and crept through the rapidly thinning jungle until he reached the barbed-wire fence that they had passed several days earlier. He parted the vegetation slowly, carefully, and studied the beach ahead of him.

At first there seemed to be nothing except the brown sand and a faint line of phosphorescence in the water where the surf broke. Behind him, a crescent moon reflected off the water. Then, far to the right, Tynan saw a man walking along the surf. He seemed to be carrying a rifle, but the distance was too great and the night not bright enough for him to be sure. It could be a native with a fishing pole or a poacher with a club.

Jones crawled over to him and reported, "Ship is in range. Said they would dispatch a whaleboat on our order. Take it about thirty minutes to get here after we ask for it."

"Okay," said Tynan. "Wait one on the boat." He rubbed his eyes gently and then stared back at the beach. The man had disappeared now. Maybe he had gone back the way he had come.

Then, from that direction, Tynan heard a snatch of conversation before the engine of a vehicle rumbled to life. There was a grinding of gears, a bang from a backfire, and then the sound of an engine retreating. It quickly faded away.

At that moment Sterne reappeared. "Looks like a squad of them on the beach about a hundred meters from here. Couple of men speaking Russian and a couple of them talking French."

"Sounds like the Soviet anticipated our move," whispered Tynan.

"How could he know which stretch of beach?" asked Sterne. "We didn't even know that."

"Probably covering it in the most likely places. Hell, most of the coastline is rock and cliffs. All he has to do is watch the beaches."

"So we just sneak between them," said Sterne. "Slip into the water and swim away."

"That seems to be the smart course," said Tynan.

"But?" asked Sterne. "You said that like you have something else in mind."

Tynan nodded. "Let's wait for Boone to return and see what he says."

They didn't have to wait long. Boone came back a few minutes later and said, "Beach ends about a hundred meters south of here. It changes into a rocky coastline that is a couple of feet above the tide line. We could get down it and onto a boat if we had to."

"Why would you say that?" asked Tynan.

"There are people on the beach. I couldn't see much, just a couple of them moving around in the shadows, but I assume they're waiting for us."

"Kind of a wild assumption," said Tynan, "but probably an accurate one. Okay, here's the deal. That Soviet guy has pissed me off. He's been dogging us since we got here. He tried to ambush us and set it up so that he could kill Hollinger if we got too close to him. I don't like it."

"So what?" said Sterne. "Not a lot we can do about it."

"I would like to do one final thing to make him look like a real jerk. Besides, we have to do something to cover ourselves while we make the extraction."

Tynan was quiet for a moment and then said, "What I want to do is have Jones radio the ship to launch the whaleboat in about half an hour. That gives us an hour to get out to it. We tell the crew to look for our flashing light in the water. We'll swim out to them. Besides, if things work out, there will be a firefight on the beach at the time, and they can home in on the shooting."

"Who's going to be in the firefight?" asked Sterne.

"If we set it up right, the guys south of here, near where the jungle touches the water, will be shooting at the guys north of us." Tynan looked over his shoulder and ordered, "Jones, make the radio call. Don't leave the radio behind when we split. We don't want the Russians to get it."

"Aye, aye, sir," said Jones. He withdrew slightly, away from the edge of the jungle and the fence, and began whispering into the microphone.

"So what's the plan?" asked Sterne.

"Three of us crawl down the beach to the water's edge and open fire on both directions. Use a full magazine and then flee into the ocean."

"Won't the muzzle flashes give them away?" asked Sterne.

"Maybe. Maybe not. But that's where the other two guys come in. We've got to get one near each group. When the shooting starts, they have to return it but put it into the other group. That way, for a moment, there will be fire coming from one group and hitting the other."

"And then?"

"Those guys have to get themselves into the water and swim out to the whaleboat."

"Okay, Skipper," said Sterne. "Who gets what job?"

"I'll take the group to the north," said Tynan. "They'll be the hardest to elude. The guy who hits the south group can retreat into the rocks just off the beach and get into the water from there."

"I'll take them," said Sterne.

"Right, thanks." He looked at Jones and said, "You're going to have to crawl down the beach with that damned radio strapped to your back. Once into the ocean you can dump it, but we've got to get it out of here."

"Aye, aye, Skipper."

"The timing on this is going to be critical," said Tynan.

"Give Sterne and me about fifteen minutes to get into place. When you reach the water, you open fire. We'll take it from there. Any questions?"

When no one spoke, Tynan said, "Good luck, and give us fifteen minutes."

Tynan didn't wait for anything more. He moved deeper into the jungle and stood up. He dropped all his equipment, throwing away his canteen, machete, and pistol belt. He stuffed his three spare magazines into his pockets. He jammed the combat knife that had been on his pistol belt into his boot opposite the smaller one already hidden there, wrapping the laces through the loop on the scabbard to hold it in place. That done, he began working his way to the north, moving quickly and quietly, listening for signs that the Soviets were near him.

He made the hundred meters in ten minutes. He got down to his belly, crawled to the fence, and looked out onto the beach. Directly in front of him he could see a couple of men sitting at the high-tide line. Both had their backs to him, so that he couldn't tell if they were Soviets or members of the local militia. Farther to the north he could see the snout of a truck sticking out of the jungle, the bed hidden by the bushes and trees. Standing around it were four or five men. Tynan crawled along the fence line, toward the truck.

The men seemed to be engaged in some kind of game of chance that involved a great deal of low murmuring. They were paying no attention to what was going on around them. Tynan crept forward, eased himself under the truck, and then stopped. Suddenly he realized that he had found the perfect position. His back was covered by the tires. The men around the hood wouldn't be able to see him. He could fire down the beach and suddenly the men near him would be watching there, not looking under the truck.

As quietly as he could, he backed up so that he was on the rear side of the front tires. He pulled one of the spare magazines from his pocket and set it on the inside of the tire where he could reach it quickly and easily. Then he waited, watching the beach.

Although he knew they were there, he never saw Boone, Ross, or Jones crawl down the beach. He knew they were in position when the staccato burst of an AK shattered the night. Tynan saw the muzzle flashes from one of the weapons.

Firing erupted around him. He saw some of it directed toward the water where Jones, Boone, and Ross had been. Tynan pointed his weapon and fired a short burst in return. Then he saw the muzzle flashes of the enemy weapons at the far end of the beach. He shifted and fired into them.

All around him there was shouting as the enemy tried to figure out what was happening. There was a burst of fire from a heavy machine gun set somewhere behind him in the jungle. He could see the green tracers flashing into the night. They were directed down the beach, at the enemy there. The plan was working; they were shooting at each other.

Over him Tynan heard several rounds slam into the body of the truck, rocking it on its springs. There was a hiss of air as one of the tires was hit, and then a bubbling as a round struck the radiator. Tynan decided it was time to get out.

He reached down and grabbed the combat knife in his boot. With a single motion, he jerked it free and spun it so that he could slice the laces. He rolled to his back and cut the other boot and then kicked both of them free. He stuck the knife in the sand and ripped the socks from his feet.

He retrieved his knife, and then, with his rifle held in his right hand, he turned and crawled from under the truck. A Soviet, crouched near the front fender, turned and looked at him. Tynan swung the rifle one-handed and heard the barrel smash into the soldier's face with a satisfying crunch of bone and teeth. The man began to shriek in pain. Tynan clubbed him again, silencing him.

A man at the front of the truck turned his head to stare and yelled something at Tynan in Russian. Tynan had no idea what the man said. He swung the barrel of his rifle around and pulled the trigger. The soldier took three rounds in the head from close range. His skull disintegrated as he collapsed into the sand without making another sound.

With that, Tynan dropped the AK. He heard the windshield shatter as a round struck it. He could hear the Soviets firing. Just inside the trees he could see the muzzle flashes as the soldiers there tried to eliminate those at the far end of the beach. Tynan could see two bodies on the sand where he had seen the two men sitting. The had apparently been killed when all the shooting started.

Tynan crouched by the body of the man with the smashed jaw for a moment, studying the sand in front of him. It was a fifty-meter sprint to the water. It was doubtful he could make it without one of the Soviets seeing him. The question was, would they shoot? He decided the question was without merit. He took a deep breath and shot forward like a runner coming out of the starting blocks.

Behind him Tynan heard a shout, but he didn't stop running. He heard a change in the sound of the firing, as if someone had turned a weapon on him. He thought he heard an insect whip past his ear and realized that it was a bullet. But he didn't care, because he was almost to the water.

The shape seemed to loom out of the sand. Tynan had no idea that anyone had been that close to the tide line on that part of the beach. The man stood there, slightly hunched over, his hands out as if he were the tackle waiting for the running back. Tynan didn't hesitate. He plowed into the man, and they both went down, rolling in the sand. Tynan scrambled to his feet, switching the knife from his left hand to his right.

The man came at Tynan. Tynan feinted with the knife, dropped, and kicked the man's feet out from under him. As the enemy fell to his side Tynan leaped and plunged the knife into the man's chest. There was a momentary resistance as the knife hit bone, but Tynan twisted it and jammed it in, feeling the warm blood gush over his hand and arm. The man jerked, tried to flip Tynan off, but Tynan rolled forward, jamming his forearm against the enemy's throat. He stabbed the man again and again until he felt the tension drain from the man's muscles.

Tynan leaped to his feet, feeling the eyes of a dozen Soviets on him, unsure of who had won the fight. Tynan whooped once, as if telling them that he was on their side; then he spun and dived into the shallow water of the Atlantic Ocean.

He felt the sand scrape his chest as he reached out, swimming along the bottom. He could hear bullets churning through the water around him, and he kicked and pulled, trying to get deeper.

A minute later he surfaced, glanced quickly, and then dived back under, swimming farther out to sea. He broke through again, this time turning and looking at the beach, now a hundred yards behind him. He could see the tracers from both sides still bouncing through the air and could hear the shooting as they tried to annihilate each other. He couldn't help grinning as he watched the muzzle flashes sparkling at the edge of the jungle.

He turned and began swimming toward the whale-boat, not sure that it was out there yet because he couldn't see or hear it. He swam almost lazily, trying not to fight the ocean but to use it.

Finally, in the distance, he could hear the quiet pulsating throb of the engine as the whaleboat plowed along. Out of the corner of his eye, he saw the flash of the strobe that Ross held as a beacon. Tynan turned toward it, swimming slowly. He stopped momentarily to tread water, his eyes looking back at the coastline, but it was now silent and there were no lights along it. The Soviets had figured it all out, but it didn't matter. The whaleboat was there, and in minutes they would be on a United States naval vessel on the high seas.

16

Soviet Captain Vladimir Stepanovich Molodin stood near the high-tide line and stared into the inky blackness above the Atlantic Ocean. He thought that he could hear the distant pop of a small boat's motor, but he wasn't sure. He thought that he could see the running lights of a capital ship, but he wasn't sure. At the moment, he thought a lot of things that he couldn't be sure of.

Slowly he turned. Up the beach in the tree line was a truck which still burned brightly, its fuel set on fire by one of the tracer rounds fired by the men who had been at the other end of the beach. Lying near it were the poncho-covered shapes of another three of his men. He didn't know who had killed them. It might have been the Americans when they made their break, or it might have been the major's men who had started firing indiscriminately at them. No, he decided, that wasn't fair. His men had opened fire too, and five of the major's men were dead also.

He started back toward the jungle. He saw a man angling at him and in the flickering light of the burning truck could tell that it was the major. He halted and waited for the black man to join him.

"We seem to have failed again," said the major, his voice betraying no concern.

"Yes," said Molodin. "Failed again."

"So," said the major, clapping Molodin on the shoulder, "what will happen to you now?"

"I will return to the Soviet Union and try to explain what happened at the plane and here on the beach." Molodin turned so that he could look at the major. "And I will try to convince my superiors that the failure was the result of working with the locals instead of our glorious and efficient KGB."

There was dead silence for a second, and then the major burst out laughing. "And I," he said, "will explain to my president that it was the interference of the outsiders that caused us to lose the American plane and that caused the deaths of my men."

Molodin started walking back up the beach. "Will you have any luck with that?"

"Of course. Our president distrusts everyone with a white skin. He is a racist, pure and simple, and I will use that to save myself. I have the perfect scapegoat for my failure, for it was actually your failure. There was nothing that I could do about it. And you?"

"I do not know, my friend. It depends on the mood in the Politburo. They may be inclined to think that my mission was sabotaged from within, and since all my soldiers are loyal, it must have been the natives who were to blame. They are racists too, in their own way. They will not believe that the Americans could sweep in here and do nearly everything they wanted when they wanted."

"They were not entirely successful," the major reminded him. "We did kill one of them."

"No, my friend, we really did not. He sacrificed himself to save his friends. Of course, my superiors will not believe that. It is probably best to forget that we killed one of the Americans. It is probably best to claim a clean sweep for them. Makes it just that much more obvious that they had help. Local help.''

"Yes, you are probably right about that." The major stopped walking as they reached the poncho-covered bodies. "You will need transport back to the airport?''

"Yes, as soon as it can be arranged."

The major started to walk away, stopped, and turned back. "Did you learn anything useful from the air-craft?''

"I'm afraid that the scientists and engineers had almost no time to study it. They saw evidence of microtechnology, and they picked up some scraps of metal that might teach us something, but I'm afraid that we learned virtually nothing.''

"Ah. I see," said the major. "And those people are back at the airport?''

"I am sure they are by now. Waiting for the flight out," said Molodin.

"Yes. Well, I shall arrange transport for you and your men. I won't be able to accompany you, I'm afraid. I must explain to my president how this dis-aster came about and what an incompetent bastard you are.''

Molodin laughed. "Make it good, my friend. Make it good.''

It had taken the bouncing of the whaleboat as they headed for the ship to convince Tynan that they were free of the enemy and the African coast. Jones, Boone, and Ross had already been on board when he had arrived, and seconds later they heard Sterne calling to them. When he was hauled in, the coxswain came about. As they rode back to the ship Sterne revealed that he had taken a round just under the armpit during the firefight in the jungle clearing but hadn't mentioned it because he didn't want to slow them down. The wound wasn't deep, had bled itself clean, and didn't hurt him much. Jones broke out the first-aid kit, using it until they could get Sterne up to the sick bay.

At the ship they hadn't had to climb a cargo net to board because there was a ladder in place. They sent Sterne up first, followed by Ross, Jones, Boone, and finally Tynan. He was surprised to see a large group of men, most of them in Navy uniforms but a couple of them wearing suits and ties. Tynan wondered how comfortable the suits would be in a tropical environment; from what he could see, the men looked miserable.

The captain appeared out of the crowd and said, "Welcome aboard, gentlemen. If you'll accompany me to the wardroom, I believe that there are a few men there who want to speak with you."

"I've got a wounded man," said Tynan.

"He'll be fine," said the captain. "Our ship's surgeon is quite good and he'll keep us posted." The captain held out a hand and said, "This way, gentlemen."

They headed up a companionway. One of the ship's officers opened the hatch to the wardroom and then stepped back out of the way. Tynan and his men entered. Sitting at the table was Wheeler, the CIA man from London. Next to him was Conway, wearing his military uniform, his colonel's eagles flashing, and behind them, on the old settee, was Bobbi Harris.

Tynan glanced at her. She smiled and raised her eyebrows in greeting.

"Sit down," said Wheeler. "We have a problem here."

Without a word, Tynan collapsed into one of the chairs. He picked at the tablecloth as if he had found something fascinating on it. He turned and looked up at the captain. "Sir," he said, "we've had nothing to eat for quite a while, and that was C rations."

"Of course," interrupted the captain. "I wasn't thinking. I'll have the cooks rustle something up for you." He snapped his fingers at an ensign.

"Before you get too comfortable," said Wheeler, "tell me what happened out there. Did the Soviets see the plane?"

"See it? Yes," answered Tynan. "Get anything useful from it? I doubt it."

"Doubt it? Why?"

"Mr. Wheeler, the briefing you provided was not as complete as it could have been. There were holes in some of the equipment bays. We don't know whether that equipment had been removed by the Soviets or if it was missing when the plane took off. And speaking of Soviets, someone should have given us more information to work with. How far were we allowed to go? I had to make assumptions in the field."

"Ah yes," said Wheeler looking toward the sky as if he could count on divine guidance. "How far could you go? I would think engaging in firefights with the Soviets was a step too far. I would say that engaging in fights with the indigenous population was too far."

Tynan didn't like the tone of Wheeler's voice. He slammed a hand to the table and said evenly, "Then that information should have been given to me before we left on the mission. I initiated none of those fights. If we hadn't engaged in them, the Soviets would have been in possession of the plane and you could debrief us in Moscow."

"Let's remember where we are," cautioned Wheeler. "And let's remember who you're talking to."

Tynan sighed. He rubbed a hand over his face. "Just ask your questions."

For the next thirty minutes, Tynan and his men told Wheeler and Conway everything that had happened. They went into great detail, leaving out nothing. Wheeler interrupted only a couple of times to ask specific questions. He would nod at the answers, and Conway made a few notes in a small notebook that he had pulled from a pocket. The food arrived, and Tynan stopped talking while it was served, but as soon as the cooks left, Tynan began again. Jones added some information, and Ross explained what he had seen when he had finished rigging the explosives.

During the debriefing, Tynan kept glancing at Bobbi, wondering what she was doing on the ship. She sat quietly, sometimes studying the deck under her feet and sometimes watching Tynan. She had on a fashionably short skirt and was teasing Tynan by crossing and recrossing her legs slowly.

When Tynan and his men finished outlining the mission, Wheeler got to his feet. He paced along the table several times, a hand stroking his chin, as if deep in thought. Finally he spun and faced Tynan. "Not good enough," he said. "You really fucked it up."

"Fucked it up?" said Tynan, his voice rising. "Fucked it up? We blew up the goddamned plane before the Soviets could learn anything from it. We captured two dozen of them and let them go the first chance we got. We went straight in and got straight out. How in the hell did we fuck it up?"

"Don't be stupid, Tynan," Wheeler shot back. "It was supposed to be a covert mission. There was nothing covert about it."

"You have some specific criticisms," snapped Tynan, "you let me know what they are. Or if you have some specific questions, you ask them. If not, then why don't you let me and my men eat our dinner and get cleaned up.''

"Don't you go giving me instructions," said Wheeler. He leaned forward, both hands on the table, so that he was staring down at Tynan. "You're here to take them.''

"Tynan is right," said Conway quietly. "Frank, we've gotten everything we need now. We can file our report.''

Wheeler turned his head slowly until he was staring at Conway. He straightened up. "You're right. I just hate incompetence no matter where I find it." With that, he stormed from the room, nearly shoving an ensign to the floor.

"Well," said Tynan.

"Yes. Well," responded Conway. "Lieutenant, I'm going to need a complete report on your activities. Everything that happened. I'm afraid there will be some awkward questions to answer.''

Tynan slumped in his chair, suddenly tired. Tired of it all. Tired of fighting with bureaucrats who couldn't see beyond their own petty problems. Tired of doing jobs where he had only a small part of the information he needed. Tired of the responsibility of acting in foreign countries, on his own, with no one to blame but himself.

"Okay," said Tynan. "Just how much trouble am I in this time?''

Conway snapped his notebook shut and jammed it into his pocket. Slowly, deliberately, he clipped his pen to the inside pocket of his military jacket. "Not much," he said. "For all the problems with the locals and the Soviets, you did get the plane destroyed before it could be exploited by the Soviets. You did it with a minimal amount of fuss. I don't think that the Russians or the local government will be inclined to protest. Too many embarrassing questions to answer.''

"Then we're in the clear?''

"Yes," said Conway. "I would think so. You'll probably be sent back to the SAS school to finish the training there." He looked at Ross. "You'll probably be sent back to your ship to complete your tour.''

"All right!" said Jones, slapping the table. "All right!"

Conway slid back his chair and stood. "I might remind you that everything that has happened in the last few days is classified. I don't want you talking about it to anyone. You have never been to Africa, you have never seen the Blackbird and, in fact, don't know what it is, and you never met me or Wheeler. These last few days just never happened.''

"Suits me fine,'' said Tynan.

"No matter what Wheeler says,'' added Conway, "you people did a hell of a job. A tough job with very little information. A hell of a job." He left the wardroom, taking the ensign with him.

With everyone except Boone, Jones, and Ross gone, Bobbi got to her feet. She stepped close to Tynan and put a hand on his shoulder. "Glad it worked out,'' she said.

That was not exactly the greeting that he had hoped for, but then Jones, Boone, and Ross were still present. "What the hell are you doing here?" he asked.

She slipped into a chair beside him. "Wheeler thought he needed some secretarial help and, since I was already briefed on the mission, he dragged me along. Not that I objected, except to be classed as a secretary. But all I've had to do was some light typing, and that keeps him happy.''

"And I'll bet the sailors have been happy too.''

She smiled broadly. "Let's just say that I've had all the help I could use. Have you finished eating?"

Tynan looked at the remains of the sandwich on his plate. "Yeah. I've finished."

"Good. Let's get out of here. I have a tiny little cabin all to myself. I'd like to show it to you."

Jones rocked back in his chair and patted his stomach as if he had just finished a seven-course meal. "Yeah," he said, looking at Ross. "I've a cabin to myself. I'd like to show it to you."

"Jones, you're bucking for a leave in the brig," said Tynan.

"Didn't mean anything, Skipper. Just wondered how you managed to get your friend down here and neglected the needs of your men. Not the best way for a skipper to operate. Forgetting about his men."

Tynan got up. With Bobbi, he moved to the hatch. "Let's just say that rank has it privileges and let it go at that."

"Aye, aye, sir." In the companionway, Bobbi grabbed him and molded herself to him. "God! I've missed you."

"That cabin you mentioned?"

She took his hand and pulled him along. "We don't have to come out until sometime tomorrow," she said. "Late in the day. Maybe early evening."

Tynan let himself be dragged down the companionway by her, watching her, studying her long legs, her long hair. Everything about her. He decided that he didn't want to come out of the cabin until late the next day. Maybe early evening.

They didn't.

by Steve Mackenzie

THE WORLD'S MOST RUTHLESS FIGHTING UNIT, TAKING THE ART OF WARFARE TO THE LIMIT — AND BEYOND!

SEALS #1: AMBUSH!   75189-5/$2.50US/$3.50Can
Under attack in Vietnam, Fire-Support Base Crockett appears doomed— until the SEALS drop in.

SEALS #2: BLACKBIRD   75190-9/$2.50US/$3.50Can
When a top-secret SR-71 crashes deep in the African jungle, only the SEALS can race the Russians to pick up the pieces.

*and more exciting action adventure
coming soon from Avon Books*

SEALS #3: RESCUE!   75191-7/$2.50US/$3.50Can
SEALS #4: TARGET!   75193-3/$2.50US/$3.50Can

KILLSQUAD

by Frank Garrett

WANTED: A world strike force—the last hope of the free world—the ultimate solution to global terrorism!

THE WEAPON: Six desperate and deadly inmates from Death Row led by the invincible Hangman...

THE MISSION: To brutally destroy the terrorist spectre wherever and whenever it may appear...

KILLSQUAD #1 Counter Attack   75151-8/$2.50 US/$2.95 Can
America's most lethal killing machine unleashes its master plan to subdue the terrorquake planned by a maniacal extremist.

#2 Mission Revenge   75152-6/$2.50 US/$2.95 Can
A mad zealot and his army of drug-crazed acolytes are on the march against America...until they face the Killsquad.

#3 Lethal Assault   75153-4/$2.50 US/$3.50 Can
The Fourth Reich is rising again, until the Hangman rounds up his Death Row soldiers for some hard-nosed Nazi-hunting.

#4 The Judas Soldiers   75154-2/$2.50 US/$3.50 Can
A madman seeks to bring America to its knees with mass doses of viral horror, but Killsquad shows up with its own bloody cure.

#5 Blood Beach   75155-0/$2.50 US/$3.50 Can
The Hangman and his Killer crew go halfway around the world to snuff out a Soviet/Cuban alliance seizing control in Africa.